A THIRTEEN-STORY VIEW

!((!
Published by Mad Zebra Press
143 Saint Louis Avenue
Buffalo, New York 14211

The stories "Matters of Taste" and "Blankets" received a Lois and Willard Mackey Prize from National Book Award Winner Bob Shacochis.

The story "But I'm Famous Here" previously appeared in *Lit Cannon: A Sampler from Mad Zebra Press* published in 2021.

Five of these twelve stories have been adapted by the author into one-act plays that are performed by Pass the Pine Cones Theater Company in Portland, Maine. Two of them were adapted under different titles: *Before There Were Hipsters*, which is based on "Matters of Taste", and *Angel With a Bloody Fist*, which is based on "Best in Honor". The others include "But I'm Famous Here", "Not Your Fight", and "Behind Tall Hedges".

Cover design is by Jacqueline Nasso Cooke.

First Printing, 2021

A THIRTEEN-STORY VIEW

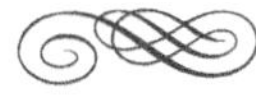

KIM SEDLOCK

Mad Zebra Press

Contents

I would like to dedicate this collection of short stories to my husband, Jason Kruger (yes, that is his real name), my stepdaughter Amelia Johnson, my step granddaughter Nathalie Johnson, my stepson Ezra Kruger, and my stepdaughter Julia Kruger.

There are no characters or storylines based on any of you, I promise. In fact, eight of these thirteen stories – all of them except for "Surgery", "Pandemic", "If Teen Novels Were Real", "The Wide Range of Subtlety Among Us", and "Everyday Horrors" – were written before I became a part of your family. But I hope that you will enjoy them immensely (as compensation for my inability to cook that well.)

A Thirteen-Story View

"Fresh, edgy, original stories of literary fiction, which flirt with both minimalism and magic realism, and which encompass themes of suffering artists, flawed relationships, breaking through denial, and embracing one's own eccentricities." – Mad Zebra Press

"Tremendously enjoyable. Confident and defined authorial voice." – Dominic Wakeford, former Senior Commissioning Editor at Harper-Collins (London, U.K.)

"Known as the 'bad girl' of literary short stories, Kim's talent is undeniable, but her approach is revolutionary. You will be fully transported." – Heather Richmond, award-winning poet

I

The Crazy Glue Factory

Local legend said that Doris's Coffee Shop was built over an Indian burial ground that contained the corpse of a great shaman. Further down the boardwalk, the gift shop cashier with the big blue Mohawk told everyone that the shaman had been able to heal a bird's wings just by singing over them. Then she spread her best shell jewelry out on the counter, as if it was somehow associated. The surfing instructor with the Brooklyn accent claimed the shaman could tell the medicinal properties of a plant just by staring at it, although clearly he had been born long enough ago that the two men never would have met. Doris herself was the one who started the rumors, however, when she claimed that the shaman's spirit had visited her in the kitchen, chanting and dancing and wrapped in a blanket of fur, and told her to add a blueberry pie to the menu. It might be called an urban myth – if Old Orchard Beach, Maine was in any way urban.

Doris's Coffee Shop was known to the locals as Oris's Coffee Shop, since she hadn't bothered to put up another 'D' for years after the last hurricane had hit. She was also the last woman in Maine to still be wearing a beehive hairdo, and she wrote personalized daily horoscopes for all her customers on the back of their paper place mats. There was another well-known story that she had chased the hotel manager next door out of her kitchen by swinging a vacuum cleaner at him after he had accused her of stealing a stack of ashtrays for her own business. That might have been an urban myth, too – 'cept it was true.

Zack looked around at Oris's new Canadian flag table cloths, and then dug into his chowder. He had lived here for all of his nineteen years. He brought his face right down over his bowl and smiled up at Miranda. He was the only person she knew who even smiled when he was eating. They had been coming there since they became friends in third grade to talk about how nothing ever happens there. Miranda lit a cigarette. A couple lobsterman at Oris's, still in their rubber chaps and knit caps and orange suspenders, had already noticed her as "that girl with the handbox." You will learn all about the handbox later, but what's important to know right now is that her own hell-fearing family, seven siblings and two parents, didn't know about her handbox, yet everyone else on the boardwalk did – she had entertained strangers for hours with it. Then again, no one in her family knew she had darkened her hair and cut it at a slant two weeks ago. All the way through school, she and Zack had been the shyest kids in town, although Zack had never seemed shy when they were hanging out alone. With her, he was very charismatic – maybe because she was the only girl in Old Orchard Beach that he had never had a crush on, and she was also the girl who had started him smoking cigarettes, but he never told her that he was doing it to lose weight. Her chunky silver rings clanked together as she handed him a smoke after his chowder. They both leaned back and watched the smoke curl into a fragile, floating, white ribbon.

"You will love the new album I just bought on vinyl," he told her. "It combines your obsession with Greek myth with the most incredible violin music. I can't wait to play it for you."

She put on an army jacket that she had decorated with a Sharpie, and he flipped his hood up. They walked down the creaking wooden planks with seagulls accosting them for leftovers, and turned down Zack's street. His mom was a waitress at Oris's. This wasn't her shift, but she was out getting stoned with her new boyfriend and would probably come home at sunrise to change quietly back into her uniform. Now that he was nineteen, Zack lived in the basement.

Miranda was pretty sure that no one in the world owned anything akin to her handbox, but Zack did have something in that basement that was highly unique. It was a kaleidoscope camera. He had inherited it from his grandfather. It operated as a kaleidoscope that formed symmetrical colorful blob pictures when you turned its lens – and it also operated as a camera, which recorded whatever was right in front of it, but with the blob pattern layered on top of the shot, like a translucent tapestry that veiled reality. Neither of them had ever heard of another camera like this one and although Zack believed the camera took high-quality pictures, it was really *Zack* who took high-quality pictures: wrapping the blobs around an oncoming wave like a Native American blanket that was cradling it, imposing the blobs around the midnight stars and making them part of the pattern, capturing the color streaks emerging from Miranda's open mouth – the color streaks of her laughter.

Miranda sat Indian-style on his floor and listened to his new album. When the violins started, she began playing air violin at lightning speed, and then, moving her fingers away from the imaginary instrument, she began a hand-dance. One hand was spread out in front of her, kind of undulating and one hand was clenched into a fist with just her pinky sticking out and vibrating. The open hand deflated gradually as if it was losing air and being sucked inward, and the clenched fist simultaneously seemed to be scratching its own itch, the sides of fingers rubbing together as it opened slowly into a tiger claw. One hand began drumming and the other began painting an imaginary picture to the rhythm. One hand began typing by itself to the harmonies and the other tying a knot by itself, following the melody, and then they both turned over, palm up, to rest.

When she was in kindergarten, Miranda had made a handbox. She had taken a cardboard shoebox and painted it entirely white, inside and out, and then cut one of the long sides out completely for her hands and one hole in the opposite side for her flashlight. When she had finished, she had begun dancing only with her hands. The light on one side caused dancing shadows; they were the scenery for her dances. She had a dance about an old swan and a young swan at war. She had a dance about an autumn leaf caught in a tornado. She had a dance about rock-climbing with no equipment and then finally grasping a power line by accident and being electrocuted during a guitar solo.

"I should do something that's about smoke," she said, staring up at the ceiling.

Sometimes, she danced in a slave bracelet. Sometimes, she danced in sheer lace gloves. Sometimes, she danced with a piece of cookie dough on the end of each finger tip. Last year, she had gotten a small blue film that could be placed in front of her flashlight whenever she wanted to make the light blue and had learned to move her fingers as though they were underwater.

"That was funny – the lobstermen saying you're that girl with the handbox!" Zack wandered off into his darkroom for a minute and then wandered back. For some reason, he had not yet photographed her hands dancing, although he had a setting that would capture streaks of motion. He ran his hands over his gut and pinched it, as if he might somehow kill it off.

"Do you think," Miranda asked him, still staring up at the ceiling, "that seeing a movement can translate a *thought* as well as a feeling? Do you think ... that if I think about how algebra is symmetrical ... that it will translate through a hand as powerfully as the *feeling* of a spring shower can? Or how severe punctation feels?"

Zack could remember her punctuation dance – all staccato movements and military turns with her fingers. It had been like sign language done to music and with near-violent emphasis on rhythm and being in the right position at the right moment.

"I really should take some kaleidoscope photos of your work," he said.

"You've been saying that for years." She laid back on the floor and her dark hair fell away from her perfect little face. She had been so shy that her beauty had been almost irrelevant to everyone, including herself. She picked at her big scary silver rings. One of them was a gargoyle with a sword through his head.

"I have a theory about your rings, you know," Zack told her.

"Yeah?" she said, still picking.

"You put those ugly things there to guard your fingers from harm."

"Could be," she said, laughing.

"You never wear them in a hand-dance. Ever."

"No, I wouldn't."

"Then on some level," Zack said with a grin, "you must know that they're ugly."

Because it was Zack, she just laughed.

She did have to hide those rings from her parents, though, even as an adult, because she also still lived at home. Her father had come to this town from Greece, worked as a lobsterman, fallen in love with her townie mom, and used to tell her Greek myths when she was very little.

She used to love those stories. Before she or Zack turned twenty, however, Old Orchard Beach would have its own story. No one would be talking about Greek myths any more. Everyone would be gossiping about Jim Loren, an outsider who became the town's unofficial king. They would be turning over in their minds to understanding what had led to his power and how everyone had been touched by it. They would be watching him covertly, as he shopped for his groceries, memorizing the brand of watch he wore and the joke he told the clerk, and listening as he walked his golden retriever on the beach, talking softly on the phone about his stocks and sometimes about how he much loved Old Orchard Beach – and not just the beach, but the town and its people.

Jim Loren had first seen Old Orchard Beach as a very young boy, too young to even remember his own age. He was in his parents' car, staring at the ocean for the first time and listening to it. His neglected popsicle had melted all over him. The second the car stopped, he had opened the door and jumped out and run through the sand and right up to the wa-ter. There, he had frozen and let it wash over his feet, again and again. How did it do that? He had looked around at the other people on the beach and they had smiled back at him. They knew it looked like magic. They felt it, too.

Every year, his family came back – to the land without homework, without chores. His parents were calm and tan there, and they smelled like coconuts and wore flip-flops. Their dog didn't need a leash. His brown hair got natural blond highlights. He had blueberry ice cream every day, and his parents bought lobsters and let him crack his own open with a nutcracker.

When he was a teenager, he looked around for girls on the beach, but the girls seemed ugly and withdrawn to him. They all worked in the shops and as bus girls in the restaurants. They were tired and cranky and had no dreams. He wanted to help them. He wanted to give them the same life that he had here, stretching out on a woven blanket and staring at the waves. After all, this ocean was their heritage, but they had all seemed too stressed out to enjoy it.

As an adult, he told everyone that he was from there, but none of the locals recognized him. None of them knew *anyone* who had summered there, because they never ate in the same places. Jim Loren was from Philly. When he had inherited his money, though, Old Orchard Beach was where he *needed* to be. He needed a large-scale investment that couldn't lose, and he wanted Old Orchard Beach to be the town that *benefited* from it, from all the new jobs he would create and all the local business that would be generated from the factory workers. And they could trust him. He loved that beach and would never dump anything in the water; the choppy sunlight on that water was woven into his memories.

What he would create is a crazy-glue factory. Crazy glue can be used for all craft projects and in many small repairs; crazy glue never goes out of style; everyone owns a tube. Why should all the stores in and near Old Orchard Beach be the stores paying extra for all that shipping? They could get it much cheaper with his factory there, and he could ship to other places instead.

It was too late to raise his daughters there. They had suffered, losing their mother to cancer so young, and he would make sure that, with his profits, he sent them both to the best schools they could get into. Every beating he had taken from his father was now rewarded with his father's money. He would put most of it into this factory and he would make it work.

He rubbed some saltwater droplets off his diver's watch. It was nice to be back there. This was where he had learned to sail. This was where the driftwood for his homemade driftwood candle-holder had come from. This was where he had his first kiss – on this beach at night; where he had first tasted French fries with meat gravy and melted mozzarella. He couldn't remember what the Canadians called that. It was the only place he had ever flown a kite, laughing wildly as his kite string got tangled into his brother's. Also lost to cancer, his brother's presence seemed to be splashed all over this beach. Until he saw the exact spot, he had forgotten how they built sandcastles late into the night and about their night-fishing on the pier together.

All those sand castles had washed out to sea, but he had built something more permanent once. He had built his own lobster trap out of driftwood and left it lying on the fishing pier for anyone to claim.

He wandered down to that old seafood restaurant on that big old boat where they used to celebrate his birthdays. He made sure to give the valet a twenty, even though he wasn't driving. He brushed the sand off his simple black tie and took out *The New York Times*. Even though he'd gone to school in Philly, the *Times* had the best international coverage.

The next day, Jim Loren stood on the veranda of their fancier hotel and gave a speech. He wore his bluejeans for it, and the townies noticed his clear blue eyes, their sincerity, and his calloused hands. He had jobs that would give higher salaries than anything in town. He had jobs that would allow them to learn management and quality control. He had jobs that would make them more secure staying right where they all already were, leaning back in their beach chairs and listening to the waves break. Not one single local recognized Jim from having been a kid there in the summers, but one by one, the whole town sat in a chair across from him and interviewed to work in his crazy-glue factory, and one by one, they all rolled out of bed and walked in a big, tight pack toward his smoke stacks, every morning until they each had two houses – one that that they rented out, and they each had tuition put away for their kids, and they each had fancy titles that they would call each other for fun when they hung at Oris's and got their daily horoscopes written out for them on the back of the paper place mats.

Zack and Miranda worked there, too. They started out in the same department, so that they could see each other every day, but she was faster with her hands than he was and so they transferred him to something different. Zack bought a whole bunch of new toys – a jet ski and a motorcycle – and Miranda gave a lot of her money to her family. Her parents had a time with all those kids still at home, so she was able to make a difference there. Jim Loren kept everyone entertained by putting in a state-of-the-art gym with a heated pool – right inside the factory – and every year, he threw a big party at his favorite restaurant on that big old boat and all the drinks were on him.

Some of the folks who had come into the lowest-rung jobs had stayed in the lowest-rung jobs, Jim had noticed, and he began strategizing ways to help them rise. He could always throw an ad in the paper and get more folks on the assembly line. But he wanted the workers who had been loyal to him to get themselves promoted somehow. He began observing their lives more closely. They spent a lot of time talking amongst themselves and laughing at practically nothing. He estimated that they thought about their work at the factory less than the higher-ups thought about it. He could see their focus drift away from what they were doing.

He could help them. It was all a manner of greater focus and of time management. After all, if he didn't help them, they might never succeed.

One of the initiatives that he devised toward this end was a donation drive toward founding a town museum. At first, people donated all the expected items – black-and-white photos from the town's early years, some antique furniture and antique tools – but he gave a speech about wanting items that were unique, to make their museum different from all other museums. What he really wanted, though, was all the silly distractions gone. He wanted that old woman with the long white hair, who everyone called Granny Crab and who worked into her nineties, to give up her mandolin. He wanted the cleaning man to give up the mystery books from the 1800s that he read by candlelight to kids at the library on Halloween. He wanted the weaving looms and the flutes and the guitars and the pots of clay for ceramics. And he didn't stand much of a chance at getting any of these – until he started *buying* them from people. And at very generous prices. They say that Zack got $100,000 for his kaleidoscope camera, and that Miranda got $10,000 for a simple cardboard shoebox painted white with a missing side and a hole in it – as long as she promised to include the flashlight.

Jim Loren piled his mansion with interesting objects. He never got around to making a museum, so he filled some of his rooms with these confiscated distractions until they spilled into other rooms, and filled his whole house. He had to make paths from his bedroom to the kitchen and the bathroom and the front door. They say he lived like this for years and didn't much mind, so intent was his focus on his factory.

The way the whole town knew that is that one night, after a very long shift, Zack had one too many beers and he dropped by Jim Loren's house in the middle of the night, looking for his kaleidoscope camera. He said that his hands were calloused up pretty badly so that he didn't know that he could work it as well as he once had, but that he would trade the money back if Mr. Loren would please be so kind as to dig it up. Together, they spent the night digging through piles of everyone's private objects and when the sun rose, they still hadn't found it.

Things at the factory hadn't gotten any faster. The people at the bottom didn't seem more focused, and if anything, the atmosphere was kind of lethargic. Jim Loren, fond of the outdoors, had never spent too much time inside his own factory. He would walk through, observing everyone, sometimes taking a little interest in the bookkeeping and the inventory, and then he would leave that clanging, crowded building with its suffocating smoke, and he would walk the beaches with his golden retriever all day. Only these days, he didn't. He was afraid to leave them all there. They looked morbid, like they might jump into a vat of crazy glue and just let the whole operation go under. Jim Loren decided there was a problem with morale. He saw the deadened eyes on the assembly lines and the slouched-over sadness in the cubicles, and truly wanted to fix it, and toward this end, Jim Loren initiated The Random Redistribution Program. This one was actually advertised on their local television channel and on their local radio station: Every object that Jim had bought for the museum would be returned to a different owner at random. This was not for any type of profit for the new owners, but for fun. If you received some sculpting tools, well, then you could take up sculpting as a hobby. If you received a phonograph that played swing music, well, then you and your wife might just want to learn how to swing-dance.

Miranda was first in line at The Random Redistribution Program. She had stopped doing her hand-dances shortly after she had donated her homemade handbox. It *was* possible to do them without that box, or even to make another handbox quite easily, but there was something about the handbox she had made when was so young, something in its rough edges, in the lopsided cut. That handbox had been with her for her first show on the boardwalk when everyone had cried out, "What is THAT?!"

Miranda wondered if she might be able to continue rejecting whatever random objects Jim Loren offered her until he would finally relent and just give her the handbox back. If not, she wondered if she might get something that was very valuable to a friend or neighbor and be able to hand it over to them, to see their face light up as their most unique treasure came home to them. Neither of these things happened, however. Instead, Miranda got an embroidery kit, and instead of even opening it, she made "wanted" posters for her handbox. She sketched it and offered a reward for its return and she staple-gunned the posters to every telephone pole and bulletin board in town.

Exhausted, she met Zack at Oris's.

They were silent for a few minutes, not having much to say really. Finally, she asked him how the chowder was this week and he said it was just fine. He said he had seen a good game show on TV, but couldn't remember the name of it, and she said that her ankles were no longer swollen. For a new espresso machine, Doris had agreed to stop writing daily horoscopes on the back of everyone's place mats, but she recognized Zack and Miranda and slipped them one on the sly. Neither of them could make out her handwriting, though, and when they did, it didn't make much sense. They were silent for a few more minutes, and then they talked a little about the storm that was coming.

They walked to Zack's new condo and Miranda fell asleep in his arms, but it was mainly because she was so exhausted. In the middle of the night, she started typing with her hands, not as the beginning of a hand-dance but because she was dreaming that she was at work. Zack, however, could feel the movement of her typing hands on his back, and felt that it was a form of love. He tried to stay awake until she was finished.

The next time they met at Oris's, they made a pact. Zack would begin painting model soldiers, as those were the objects that had been randomly redistributed to him, and Miranda would begin embroidering. Miranda took out her agenda book and wrote "embroider" on her to-do list. When the time came, however, she did the dishes, watched some TV, and drifted off to sleep. Zack rolled a joint, stared at the model soldiers with disdain, and then rolled another joint. Utterly stoned, he stumbled over to Oris's by himself and sat at his usual table. "You know what?" he said to a waitress that he had never seen there before. "There used to be a shaman buried under here."

Oris's closed early that night. All of Old Orchard Beach was asleep by midnight, except for Jim Loren, who was out night-fishing on the pier with his golden retriever. Stray cats roamed the alleys behind the seafood restaurants; tiny, pointed roofs repelled some light, passing rain; and a fragile, floating, white ribbon of smoke enveloped the community. And down below it, somewhere in every home in town, balanced on its wide cap, stood a tiny bright orange tube of crazy glue.

2

Everyday Horrors

The first time that Shannon met Dahlia, she was pacing back and forth in front of Lonna's house, with a crazy scarf tied over her head. At first, Shannon thought that maybe Dahlia was talking on the phone or smoking, but she was just pacing until Shannon arrived, apparently, so they could meet each other. Shannon had been accepted to rent a room in Lonna's house one day before Dahlia had been. You would think Lonna would be there to welcome them, but she was travelling with her wife.

Lonna was a poetry professor at the local state university and she was on sabbatical this semester. She had breezed into town to interview Craigslist candidates to live in her big house in the hipster neighborhood and was already gone again. She had told Shannon over the phone that Dahlia was an exotic-looking artist, and she had told Dahlia that Shannon was a wholesome-looking couch potato, but these descriptions were based on half-hour long interviews, most of which had been spent touring the house itself and marveling that they could live in these high-ceilinged hardwood-floored rooms for such a low price.

Lonna and her wife were speeding toward New York City now, in their hand-me-down Volvo, blasting music that had just come out last week and that no one had heard yet, while Dahlia ripped the scarf off her head and threw it on the ground, then crouched down to pick it up and stayed down there while she put it back on her head in the exact same way it had been on before. Shannon watched her as she came up the street from the bus stop. "I'm Shannon," she said with a smile, the way her parents had taught her. "You must be Dahlia."

Dahlia was silent for longer than a moment, then she laughed very loudly and spun around, her vintage dress blowing up, then she laughed some more. She grabbed Shannon's hands – both of them – and said, "We are going to have so much fun living here!" Then she squeezed Shannon's hands very hard and seemed to be jumping up and down a bit.

They helped each move in and unpack and even decorate. They walked to the coffee shop at the end of the block and tried to order sushi. They made their own mixed drinks and sat out on the back patio, talking late into the night, their nearly identical long straight brown hair blowing in the breeze. They were fast friends.

The next day, Shannon went to work, tired and slightly hung over, and at lunch, she saw a text from Dahlia that had been there for a couple hours. In a long rant, it accused Shannon of stealing some of the toilet paper from their shared bathroom and stuffing it into a shared closet in clumps. Shannon thought it might be a joke, but when she called, Dahlia screamed at her and hung up. After work, Shannon knocked on Dahlia's door and Dahlia answered and said, with great pride, that she notices everything and could not be fooled. Shannon took the roll of toilet paper off the rack and brought it to her, claiming that only a tiny bit was missing since the night before, but Dahlia haughtily shook her head and slammed the door.

The next morning, Lonna was in the kitchen making coffee. She had dropped her wife off in New York City and driven back alone last night. Why? Because she had received nearly twenty long texts from Dahlia. One tried to acquire a job as House Manager, so that she could "fix the many things that have been broken by Shannon." Another tried to convey her eligibility for said job by relaying particular song lyrics. A third hinted that Dahlia would try to replace the kitchen floor with something she had fashioned herself.

Lonna showed them to Shannon over their morning coffee.

"She thinks I stole some of our communal toilet paper," Shannon told her.

"She's crazy," Lonna answered. "I am asking her to leave."

It took the requisite thirty days, but Dahlia left, after weeks of silence, and Shannon called Lonna to report that she was gone, along with all her things, and had turned in her keys. Lonna and her wife poured some champagne and Shannon drank a celebratory beer while still on the phone with them.

Then Shannon got off the phone and walked exactly fifty-three steps to her room where she slashed one ankle with her Swiss Army knife. This was all her fault. She took her blankets, used one to soak up the blood on her ankle, and threw the rest on the floor. She would sleep on the floor tonight. It was the least she could do. She stood at her window, peeling off the paint on its sill with her thumbnail, and then threw the paint chips into her blankets for added discomfort.

Shannon lived with Lonna and her wife for one year and one month, when they were in town, always laughing about Dahlia and her texts, before Lonna found a bag of Shannon's hair in a shared closet. Assuming it had been Dahlia's, she went to throw it out, but the next day, she noticed it had been fished out of the trash and was sitting on the coffee table, surrounded by beer bottle caps in a perfect circle.

3

The Grounded Tomboy

SunYee hung a half-crocheted blanket over her skis and laid on the garage floor beneath them with a flashlight between her legs. The only part of her or the skis not covered by the blanket was her dirty bare feet. As she waxed vigorously, the blanket fluttered and changed shape. She had her whole crocheting bag nearby, for her alibi. She could pretend to be crocheting and slide the skis behind the lawn mower – very quickly, if she had to.

A couple rooms to the left, her husband, Bill, was waxing his skis, too. He had them laying across the living room floor and was listening to an old record of Chinese classical music, waxing along to its exotic scales and unimaginable instruments. He was having that daydream where he climbed famous mountains in all different parts of Asia and then skied down them at top speed.

SunYee could hear the music playing and knew it would drown out the sound of her waxing, but then her foot hit a metal rake, which came crashing to the ground. Bill was too lost in his daydream to notice. He hovered over their mauve carpet. It was neutral, tasteful, not exactly like their neighbors' but not ostentatious, either. They had picked it out together. Well, he had picked it out in her presence, and she had smiled and nodded; she had witnessed his wise selection. The carpet seemed to match their wedding picture, which hung slightly crooked in its slick chrome frame, smiling back at him. They had been married at the top of White Sugar Mountain.

As an Olympic ski instructor, it had been a big joke that with this marriage, he had lost his best student *and* his only female student by marrying her and by asking her to be his stay-at-home wife. He had proposed shortly after she had begun to out-ski him. He gazed lovingly at the picture, the both of them in formal snowsuits, hers with some Korean fabric draped above her jacket, him towering above her with a bow tie, his wispy blond hair, her so dark. His music drowned out a falling box of Christmas ornaments in their garage.

SunYee loved being in the mountains. She loved the feeling of their giant, solid support; she loved their overview of all the lands beneath them. She loved the lifts scooping her off the ground, turning down new trails and meeting unpredictable terrain and handling it, weaving around moguls, making quick turns on her own instinct, the rush of racing the people near her, and most of all: jumping. She ran her pink-painted fingernails through her newly-short black hair and glanced down at her giant waterproof watch. She thought about how her thighs were thicker and more muscular than they should be, and how Bill had said that he didn't mind. She thought about how, even though her thighs were nearly hairless, her mother had screamed that she should wax them.

She knew that at any second, she could be caught. It would be devastating for Bill if she was. He believed that he had done SunYee a favor by marrying her. Now she could feel safe, in this big brick A-frame, stay home and exercise on their new mauve carpet, support the success of Bill's new Olympic team. Now she could have whichever diamond necklace was in style each season and whichever fur coats Bill favored, and be proud in church – not just for what she was now wearing, but for sitting next to Bill, the town's star athlete. Now she didn't need anything crass like courage or adventure. She certainly didn't need to be sneaking out to ski. Why would a woman from a happy home be doing that? She could nurture Bill like a child and she would be deeply happy. In fact, *he* was deeply happy just daydreaming these things for her.

Since she had begun sneaky-skiing, SunYee had waxed her skis lying down behind the rosebush and also at the crack of dawn, with them sticking out the back of her Volvo. A lot of people waxed in the ski lodge, before or after. She never did that. She had told Bill that she had the goggles for gardening and that she was using the key that tightens your bindings in her sewing project.

An hour after his Chinese symphony record had ended, Bill was out on the slopes – or rather, he was at the bottom of one, judging a race between thirty-five contestants. The woman who won towered over him in height. You could barely discern the curves on her in that black snow suit, and her head and face were entirely covered, but she had the best time of everyone – better than Bill's fastest time, too. He watched her elegant turns and her final, fearless jump. What was she like underneath there? He tried to see her eyes behind her goggles. He imagined that she might own a motorcycle and be an heiress to a great fortune. He skied alongside her and complimented her on her turns, but she moved in busy silence, placing her trophy in a special bag, balming her lips, and skiing off to sit by the fire. Within minutes, he was fussing with all of his layers in the mens' room until he finally got to his fly, unzipping it slowly as he thought about her and stroked himself. She had thrown her hips into those turns, spewing snow dust in her trail. He could feel her eyes, aroused, behind those goggles, and imagined peeling off her black snowsuit.

Bill no longer felt the thrill of skiing. It is true, however, that the best part of his day was when he zipped his fly back up and started driving home to his wife. It was euphoric to know that he was not driving home to that aggressive black-clad mystery woman, that heartless ninja of the mountains, but instead to his nurturing, gentle wife and her pleased little smile. She would have a good stew ready and some tea on the stove. She would be in her silk robe, and he would lay back, and she would bring him everything he needed, gracefully. He would play that same record again, and he would fall asleep to its lulling wisdom, its secret knowledge of tones and rests.

An hour after Bill's Chinese Symphony record had ended earlier, Sun-Yee was also out on the slopes. She had to go to the smaller resort, to avoid Bill, but she didn't mind. Radiant, she looked back over her shoulder while on the lift and then back up to the top, anticipating the feel of the snow beneath her skis, the orgasmic thrill of jumping, the power of landing. She hoped for something new and narrow and icy and challenging. She lifted the safety bar and skied off the lift.

As she turned onto a double-diamond trail, so did a short, wide man in a fur-lined parka. As she deliberately went off course a little and turned around some evergreens, so did he. As she went straight to pick up some speed, he raced right by her, but then slowed down. Together, they went carefully over an icy patch, were blinded by a snow-machine, skied right into the sun, and together, they jumped. She went first, thoughtlessly, spontaneously, a high long stretch of nothing beneath her skis, and she twisted her skis back and forth and landed seamlessly in a forward rush of love. But she looked back over her shoulder for a second and he was up there, suspended and smiling and stretching out his arms like an eagle. Without speaking, they skied into a lift line together, rode up together, and skied another trail, this one bumpier, and they took lots of little jumps while turning over the moguls. She wanted to go off-trail to race a pair of teenagers and he immediately followed. Together, they shot past them, laughing, shooting white powder into the air as they stopped.

But then, he skied off – just like that. He seemed to be headed toward the lodge. They had spent an hour together without ever speaking, a fantastic hour, but now it was time to go home. She climbed into the Volvo that she and Bill owned in different colors – hers was mauve and his was black. The man she had been skiing with climbed into a jeep. He was an old-money day-trader, thinking about driving home to his wife, a much younger, blond pre-school teacher and nothing like this crazy woman he had been skiing with. He laughed. He glanced in his rearview to see if SunYee was still staring at him but she wasn't. He liked to eat banana pancakes for dinner sometimes. Most women will judge you for something like that, he thought, and drove off to get on the highway.

SunYee put on lip balm and cranked up the oldies station. She sang along at the top of her lungs, trying to blot out the image of their living room, with its stupid grandfather clock that chimed, the glass coffee table that always had streaks on it. Bill would be asleep on the couch. He would smell like Bengay. Maybe she needed to re-decorate. Her mother had forced her to take that flower-arranging class. She tried to remember what she knew. There were principles to it – a certain balance and harmony, particular ways to blend. She felt like she was missing a lot of it. She stayed in the slow lane and arranged a bouquet in her head. She took those gaudy yellow flowers that grow in their yard and added something tiny but vibrant blue. Then she added branches of tiny, white apple blossoms around the edges. She almost missed her exit. Usually, she took the back roads to avoid Bill, but today, she was running late to make their dinner. Instead of speeding up, though, she went even slower.

Bill was only a few miles behind her. Sore and exhausted, with two beers in him, he saw something. It was off to the left, in his peripheral vision. It looked like himself. It was himself. It looked exactly as he looked right then – thirty-two, in jeans and a flannel, innocent slightly-wrinkled eyes, forehead scar, and a square Ken-doll jaw that matched his body – only in the vision, he was being propped up by a tall, faceless, glowing angel in a cashmere sweater set, poodle skirt, and saddle shoes, and with a scarf tied around her head. But she was faint and blurry, working diligently in the background. He got off the nearest exit and was driving right toward the vision now and it wasn't fading. He had to see it close up. He was completely propped-up from the angel now, and she had begun wheeling over a rolling three-step staircase, seemingly from out of the bushes, for him to climb up. He climbed it and he stood tall and looked around. The angel straightened her skirt and smiled up at him. She had SunYee's old hair, when it had been long. In his car, he was getting closer; on the staircase, he was growing taller. Then the angel bent over and arched her back and formed an even higher slope than the staircase was. He was almost there. His brakes screeched as the vision suddenly disappeared and he had to avoid driving into the billboard for a new cell phone company. Sweating, and the hairs on his head pulsing from his pounding heart, he stared into his rearview until his expression returned to normal, and then he laughed.

SunYee wouldn't know that he had gotten off a random exit because she didn't know what time he had left the slopes, but instinctively, he started driving faster. He passed every car on the highway and finally in his own neighborhood, he swerved onto his own street and pulled right in front of a slow-moving mauve Volvo before realizing that he had just cut off SunYee. He glanced into his rearview – she was fine. He pulled into his driveway and parked, ready to laugh along with SunYee about how he had just cut off his own wife.

SunYee meant to turn into their driveway as well. She could say that she had been out running an errand, or maybe that she had gotten a facial or gone to a yoga class. She slowed down for the turn, but then thoughtlessly, spontaneously, she sped up right in front of it. Her body took over and she drove toward twilight skiing, toward the trails lit up with white lights and a whole new slew of skiers jumping into the darkness.

4

But I'm Famous Here

Once upon a time, there were three very different musicians. There was an anonymous musician (whom we will actually refer to as The Anonymous Musician) – he played trombone and didn't really live anywhere in particular, although he happened to be passing through Cleveland. There was a famous musician named Drew Lawrence who played electric guitar, of course, and did not live anywhere in particular, either, although he owned many houses. And there was a neighborhood musician named Marvin who also played trombone but lived in an efficiency apartment in Cleveland. He had nothing in common at all with The Anonymous Musician, except that they both happened to play trombone and for a couple weeks, they were both in Cleveland. It's all too easy to get two trombone players mixed up with each other, but I assure you that all three of these musicians were extremely different people, from the bottom of their souls to the very tips of their fingers.

The Anonymous Musician sat in some coffee shop in Cleveland, humming to himself, oblivious of his surroundings. He scribbled on his napkin, drummed a little on the table, spontaneously wrote a whole new song, listening to the melody in his head, honoring the lyrics that seemed to be given to him, dictated to him from some invisible void that hovered just above his head, perhaps also created *by* his head. He wasn't sure and didn't care. He drank more coffee, beamed that he had a new song, one that would convey all the different dimensions of the word "transmission." He hunched over his trombone case and picked at the Greyhound sticker on it, still beaming.

There was physical transmission: how the spices one person adds to a soufflé land on another person's tongue and how their photo of their mom travels to other countries over the internet; mental transmission: how the thoughts of an eighteenth-century philosopher find an Alaskan school teacher and then through her, find a bored teenager; emotional transmission: how joy and tension are contagious in an office, at a party, in eager correspondence. Positive transmission, negative transmission – he found it all within that melody – a melody which seemed to find him, when all he was doing was staring out the window at an empty sidewalk being hit by a heavy rain. He shoved all the scribbled-on napkins into his pockets and tipped the barista a twenty. After all, she had brought the coffee that had kept him here creating during this storm. Without her, there would only be water, and then it might have been a whole different song.

The barista didn't see the twenty tucked under his cup until he was out of sight. She wanted to greet him by name the next time he came in, but realized she couldn't, because they hadn't exchanged names, although he had chattered about his bus ride and about how he loved the sound of the storm. For his first ten minutes there, in fact, he had seemed to be doing nothing but listening to it.

At the same time, several states away, Drew Lawrence stepped forward for his guitar solo. The lighting crew had changed where his spotlight happened for this arena stage, but he got into it and hit his groove, his energy peaked, the energy of thousands of onlookers fed him. He dropped to his knees in the jeans that the costume crew had torn for him and his fingers flew up and down his hundred-grand electric guitar. His sweat dripped down onto the guitar, mostly from the spotlight, and he shut his eyes. When he opened them, everyone was dancing and screaming, as far back as he could see, far back into the field in every direction, all their eyes were on him. He looked just the way he did in the poster – perfect bone structure, six-pack abs, and just the right amount of leather in his outfit. He jumped back to his feet and grinned his wild smile. There was no greater high than this.

A third musician, who was always just known as Marvin, sat on his stoop. He lived in a tiny neighborhood within a Cleveland ghetto. He didn't venture out of that tiny neighborhood much, except for work. To him, it was like a close-knit small town that happened to be situated in the midst of something larger than itself, but not necessarily greater than itself. He loved his stoop. He tuned his trombone on it every night around ten, and people would stop and chat with him. He knew so many of the people who walked down that street at night and he was happy to put down his instrument and talk with them. He wanted to hear about their days. Then he might pick up the old trombone and play some little ditty that they requested. There was no better way to spend an evening.

Meanwhile, around midnight that same night, the Anonymous Musician from the coffee shop could not sleep. He thought it was the coffee, but actually the barista had accidentally given him decaf for his order and for every refill. He was simply excited about his new song. He played it quietly near his window again and again and felt more peaceful than if he *had* slept.

The Anonymous Musician was crashing in Marvin's neighborhood indefinitely, just down the block from Marvin actually. But he didn't know or care.

Drew Lawrence returned to the stage from his dressing room, where the lights around his vanity mirror were almost as bright as the stage lights. He was followed by the costume crew who dressed him and re-dressed him quickly and accurately between acts and who wanted his current costume back. They walked a few feet behind him in circles, as he scoured the stage for his lucky bandana. It had been tied around his boot.

"We didn't want you to wear that, anyway," one of the costume crew snapped at him.

But he saw it around the wrist of someone in the lighting crew who was guzzling down some water, and he snatched it back. Then he ran to his dressing room again to meet up with security and get ushered out the door to the limo. He wore his photo face on his way out, and then opened a bottle of vodka in the back of the limo.

His entire band was in separate limos, all going to different places. He, unfortunately, was going home, and home was South Dakota, in a tiny house filled with Evangelists, where he was neither famous nor even considered a good person. He finished a quarter of the vodka bottle and checked his hands for hangnails. His fans and bandmates loved his calloused, beat-up, guitarist hands, but his mother hated any sign of hangnails. She would only forgive them if you were farming. "Hangnails are a sign of a slovenly attitude," she would say.

This would be his last limo for a week. When his stern, silent father met him at the airport, he would be in the family pick-up truck again, listening to the Christian news station and staring at flat farmland and forced into silence himself. They had no television, read no magazines, had no friends outside of their insulated church.

They didn't know that their least favorite son was famous. And, furthermore, they wouldn't really have cared. They knew he played rock music and that rock music ruined children's lives, and that was all they needed to know.

Around the same time that Drew Lawrence had been on a plane from Vegas to South Dakota, Marvin had been in a different part of Cleveland than his little neighborhood, staring at the clock on the office wall while his boss told him that he could learn to be better at filing with a little online tutoring. There were programs that taught more advanced systems of filing and then quizzed you about them, and apparently, these programs were free. What amazing luck for Marvin.

Most people his age had retired, but Marvin was a trombone-player. Two hours from now, he would be in his own neighborhood, walking into his own church for potluck supper, and everyone there knew him – he was THE trombone-player in his neighborhood. Everyone would want to sit with him, someone would pull out his chair, he would give autographs to little girls and grandmas alike, and when he took the stage in that church hall, it was silent.

For the people in his neighborhood, Marvin was the best they had ever seen live.

"After you get better with the new filing system," his boss continued, "we can work on your typing speed."

Meanwhile, The Anonymous Musician woke up and immediately put on some vinyl. Then he lay back down and just listened. It was going to be a great day. He thought he had passed a park near that coffee shop. It was going to be a very great day.

Drew Lawrence woke up in South Dakota. In that time zone, it was nine in the morning, which meant everyone else in the family had been up for four hours. He ate his oatmeal silently while his father sat at the table across from him and stared down at the rooster tablecloth. "When are you going to turn your life around and decide to make something of yourself?" his father said. One of his younger sisters ran by with his bandana tied around her doll's head. His mother was in the bedroom praying for him.

"I'm a famous guitarist," he told his father for the millionth time.

His father shook his head and told him to stop with the lies.

Drew Lawrence watched his teenage brother out the kitchen window, on his tractor. Maybe someday, my brother will "discover" me in a record store, Drew Lawrence thought and smiled.

His mother came out of the bedroom and stared at his hands. He had a new hangnail.

Drew Lawrence didn't last the entire week. He made a few calls and booked a driver to Minneapolis, a city he had never been in before. Less than an hour in downtown Minneapolis, though, and he was at a party in a fancy hotel with hordes of adoring fans he had never met before, yet who all had his lyrics memorized. He sang along with them and stared out the window at the city below.

Marvin lived alone in an efficiency apartment with a roach problem. He had lived in that same spot for most of his life. I have certainly sacrificed everything for my art, Marvin thought to himself, as he pulled his bed out from the couch. His church supper "gig" had ended an hour ago and would happen again next week. He couldn't sleep and he took his trombone out of its stickered-up case and sat on the edge of his bed with it and played an hour on his own.

All the while, there was something big that Marvin didn't know. You see, while Marvin was a good trombone-player for his church – and he was even a good trombone-player for his neighborhood – Marvin wasn't a good trombone-player. He was just okay.

Meanwhile, The Anonymous Musician put his case on the grass. He was already tuned-up, so he just started playing. With a great sense of euphoric release, he played for six hours without realizing it.

On his way out of the hotel, Drew Lawrence saw a fake Greek vase in the lobby that was the exact same type and colors as his parents owned: twice the size of an ordinary vase, formed like an angular hourglass, white and bright blue, depicting the Greek muses. It was something they had saved for and ordered from a catalogue. It had been around for most of his childhood, though. It had been filled with gaudy orange flowers at their Thanksgiving dinners when the men had sung the high school football songs and filled with a dozen long-stem red roses when his sister had her toddler ballet recital. That was back when he was one of them, when they could talk. He walked up to it and ran his hands over it and cried with no sound. The only thing he loved besides his family was being a rock star. But he had loved it so much that it had brought him into an entirely different world, one from which he couldn't exactly return – even when he did return. He could never really be present at their table any more. His secret life was just too big to share with them. Anyway, they didn't want to know.

"Drew Lawrence!" a tiny pink-haired groupie shrieked and ran up to him.

"Hi," he said softly and tried to feel her love.

Marvin woke up to the alarm and dreaded going to his office job.

He was a celebrity in his own neighborhood and yet those office people treated him like he was a loser. Today would be different, he vowed.

He had a tin drawer in his efficiency kitchen that was filled with all his schwag: recordings of all his music, gig posters, and a newspaper article clipping with his picture and a brief review. Today, he would bring all of it into the office and show it to them.

And he did. He showed it all to each of them a couple times, because he couldn't understand their silence. He didn't realize that they thought he was self-promoting and delusional.

Drew Lawrence went back to work, too. He felt at home again when he was centerstage. He felt fully himself and known. Everything he thought and felt and did and experienced was shared with a million people he had never met before. He reached his hand into the ray of the stage light and tried to grasp it.

Marvin, though, had the same experience at Bingo. That was an impromptu gig for him. They didn't expect him there that night. There was Mrs. Crow, who had encouraged him in third grade, when she first heard his music, and there was Jameson who had tried to learn trombone but quit, and there was Lindsay, the first woman to be wooed by his playing. When Marvin played that night at Bingo, he put on the best show he had all year, and when they clapped and screamed for him, he was the real Marvin again.

Next week, he was due to speak at the local junior high and play a little there. He only hoped he could inspire the next generation with his playing.

He made his way home from Bingo, passing by the park. There was an excellent street-performer there that night – a trombone-player. Crowds had gathered around him and were dancing and clapping along. Marvin wasn't impressed and just kept walking. Whatever those crowds heard, he couldn't hear it. And when he got home, he went to sleep with a smile on his face.

Courtesy of his band's booking agent, Drew Lawrence happened to be in Cleveland that night, too. And he happened to pass that same trombone player.

And Drew Lawrence was also unimpressed; that player had no showmanship, sounded very outdated, and he wasn't very handsome, either. He was wearing suspenders, for Christ's sake. Drew Lawrence hurried along – he was on his way to another hotel room to meet with a reporter. Later on, he too fell asleep with a smile on his face.

That trombone player in the park told stories with the notes, created colors with the melodies, bared soul. Most people in a hurry stopped. Everyone smiled; everyone moved. People who didn't like trombone music, people who didn't usually like a particular cover – they all stayed until the end. He seemed to be at one with the music. It seemed to emanate out of him as if it was being created spontaneously from the deepest part of him.

He had played his whole life – for his family, for his co-workers, for strangers, for himself.

Everyone in the crowd was still thinking about his music as they got home – how it affected them, how it tied in with their lives, what it made them picture. And then they each realized that none of them even knew his name – they only knew his work. And they all fell asleep with smiles on their faces.

5

Matters of Taste

Jeanine had always been irritated by scarves – not the kind of scarves that are made of wool and are meant to keep your neck warm in winter, but the kind that are made of silk or cotton. Sure, they come in some jazzy patterns – paisley, embroidered, that red-and-white kind that you see tied around dogs' necks in 70s pictures. Even the world-famous fashion designers have produced their own "signature" scarves, but Jeanine's question was: Does anyone know what to do with them? Because tying them around your neck was not the answer. First of all, they make it look like you're trying to hide something: a scar, a stain, a big hole near your neckline. And secondly, they feel like bibs. Every time, Jeanine put one on, she was reminded of her mother waving a spoonful of strained beets in front of her face, trying to pretend it was an airplane. But Jeanine thought the biggest issue was worthiness. You have to be worthy to wear a scarf. You have to be one of those put-together women who knows what she is going to wear the night before and color-coordinates everything that touches your skin. Otherwise, it doesn't look right. People can tell you're faking.

"Why did you take off the scarf I gave you?" Rob demanded. "I thought you were going to wear it to the movie. I knew you didn't like it." They were sitting around his apartment, drinking beer and playing gin rummy amid the thrift-shop blankets and piles of old magazines that covered the floor. Rob could never bear to throw anything out.

"Rob, it's hot. My neck is starting to sweat. I'll wear the scarf some other time."

Rob was one of these men who got neurotic about his presents. When Jeanine first met him, he was shopping for his girlfriend Gina. Jeanine had sat behind the counter in the lingerie department and watched him comb every aisle twice, stopping, squinting, lifting up a ceramic deer, a plastic photo album, and placing them all back on the shelves, until he finally made his way to the lingerie department. "What's your favorite thing in the store?"

"I would never shop here," she told him frankly.

For a moment, he looked taken aback. Then he laughed. "Your boss know you say that to customers?"

"You think my boss shops here?"

Jeanine was fired a week later, but it didn't matter. She was still living with her family then and there was simply no connection between the hours that she worked and the food that she ate. By now, however, she figured she should appreciate money, having lived as a starving art student/waitress for two years. She should be able to look at that huge silk scarf with the scene of a country farmhouse printed on it that Rob probably spent hours picking out and realize that it cost him at least ten dollars. Big spender, that Rob. She supposed she wouldn't have to feel too guilty if she "accidentally" lost it. After all, aside from her feeling about scarves in general, this particular one thar Rob had chosen was garish, cheap-looking, and – well – just utterly tasteless.

She grabbed her leather, Rob grabbed his old jean jacket, and they headed out the door and down the sidewalk to Cinema Twelve.

"I've heard this is really good," Rob told her. "Troy loved it." (Troy and Liam were a team of famous movie critics.)

"What about Liam?" she asked him.

"You know Liam – he never likes anything. He's too picky."

"There's no shame in having discriminating taste, you know." She looked down and realized the corner of the scarf was sticking out of her purse. She unzipped a little and stuck it back in.

When she looked up again, she saw two men carrying a divan down the sidewalk. It was the divan, not the men, that caught her eye. It was red velvet with a long back that flared out wide at the end like a throne. The curling shape of its frame was so precise, the intricate carvings on its legs so impressive, and everything about its proportions so absolutely correct that she stopped walking to study it.

"Well, it doesn't hurt anyone but Liam," Rob answered. "He's the one who can only enjoy ten percent of what he sees. I'd rather be a little more inclusive myself." His voice trailed off as he kept walking, not even noticing the divan, and she had to run to catch up.

Breathless, she mumbled, "Rob, it's not like Liam decides to be that way. He can see more flaws in films than your average joe because he knows more *about* films." Jeanine almost followed the divan right past the theater, but Rob grabbed her arm.

"Two for Everyone's Invited," he told the ticket lady.

"It's all sold out," she told him. "You can try back at nine, if you like."

Rob turned and looked at Jeanine. "Second choice?"

Jeanine scanned the billing board, but all the titles looked so hokey.

"How about Only the Chosen?" Rob suggested. "It starts in five minutes, so we won't have to wait."

"Great," she lied. Sounds ominous, she thought.

Rob paid, they entered the dark red-carpeted lobby and bought popcorn and Good 'N Plenty and one huge Coke to split. Jeanine went to the ladies' room and walked down the row of empty stalls, flipping open doors to find the cleanest toilet.

While she was washing her hands, a mother came in with a young child. She couldn't have been more than eight or nine, but she was the most sophisticated-looking young girl that Jeanine had ever seen. The girl had waist-length black hair and she was wearing a cameo brooch. How odd to see a child in a brooch.

Her mother squatted down eye-level with the child. "Are sure you don't have to go?" she asked.

The girl nodded.

"Okay, then, wait right here. Mommy'll be right out."

Jeanine reached for a paper towel from the dispenser but found it empty. She turned to the little girl. "Is that your mother's brooch?" she asked.

"No," the little girl replied, speaking slowly as if Jeanine was the child. "It was a present from my father."

Jeanine was about to smile and say how very pretty it was, but before she could get the words out, the little girl said, "Do you like it?"

She didn't sound insecure at all – just very casual, as if the only importance of Jeanine's opinion was as a topic for small talk.

Jeanine did not know what got into her then. Maybe it was the beer or the having missed the right movie or the way the little girl was looking at her, so calm and condescending. Jeanine looked at the pin with its rose background, encased with tiny silver intricately patterned borders, and its perfect ivory profile of a lady in a flowing robe with layers of folds that fell in waves. It was art, really. She looked right at it and lied. "No," she told the girl, effecting a tone that was carefully apologetic. "But that doesn't mean you can't enjoy it."

The girl didn't crumble a bit. "I do enjoy it." She fingered it. "I'm sorry you can't like it, too. I like your scarf."

Jeanine looked down and realized the intrusive brightness of her scarf poking out again. Humiliated, she stuffed it back into her purse.

At the same time, the girl's mother flushed and emerged from the stall. She was wearing an expensive suit, just enough gold jewelry, and her black hair was in a flawless French braid. She glanced at Jeanine sideways in the mirror. "You look so familiar," she informed Jeanine and, turning to fully face her, she added, "Are you a waitress at The Tropical Cove?"

"No," Jeanine lied, glaring. "I am an art student at the university." Realizing that her hands had been dry for several minutes, she turned sharply and left.

Rob had already chosen their seats. She joined him during the previews. She kicked her boots up onto the empty seat in front of her and tried to relax.

Only The Chosen was about a woman who wrote book reviews and neglected her cat. But the movie was mostly about her love life. She had been dating the same man for two years. He was an older television salesman who thought that books were detracting from television viewership. He chose everything for her from her dinner to her perfume and she was secretly never satisfied with anything he chose. Toward the beginning of the film, she began seeing another man as well: the manager of an art gallery. He bought her a bottle of the finest champagne, the kind you have to go to an auction to buy, and he helped her to redecorate her apartment.

"I think this must be based on a Harlequin Romance," Jeanine whispered to Rob.

"Shh!" he hissed.

Finally, the woman chose the television salesman. She came to this decision in a rather pathetic climax scene wherein – get this – she spied on him when he thought she was taking a bath and she saw him playing with her cat – which had almost starved to death and certainly had never been played with – and she was touched. It ended with their cheesy outdoor wedding. Jeanine almost puked. Rob cried.

"That was an awful film," she told him. She thought he should be enlightened since he obviously couldn't tell himself. They had left the theater and were walking back to her place.

"That was a very touching film," Rob mumbled. He was barely listening; he was watching an old woman trying to cross a busy street with a squirming poodle in her arms. The poodle had a cast on each of its hind legs.

"Guess she's taking Lucky for a walk," Jeanine said.

They were silent for a block.

She tried to be diplomatic. "The cinematography in the camping scene was impressive."

Rob didn't answer.

"The background music was good, too," she added. "I would definitely buy the soundtrack."

"Maybe I'll get it for you," Rob mumbled bitterly, "as a present."

She felt her purse with her hand to make sure her scarf wasn't sticking out. "Look, Rob, what do you want me to say – it was the best film I've seen all year?"

"You don't have to say anything. You are not the World Judge of Movies."

"How can I not judge it? I just sat looking at it for an hour and a half. You judged it, too. You just judged it generously is all."

Rob shook his head at her and was silent. She hated it when he was silent.

"Look," she told him, "if I could, say, have lunch with the director, I would be very constructive in my criticism. I know it's very difficult to make films and I – "

"You know that?!" Rob shouted. "How do you know that?! You're a waitress and an art student! You don't know anything about films! Nothing!"

"Rob, movies are made for the public, AND I AM PART OF THE PUBLIC, GODDAMMIT!" She didn't even care that she was making a scene. He is just so arrogant sometimes, she thought.

She walked the rest of the way home alone. As soon as she got home, she took out her paints. She slammed all the jars on the table as she unpacked them from the shoebox and then she just sat in front of them for a while, trying to slow her breath and clear her mind. She warmed up on the back of an embarrassing sketch she had done of a vase – one of her first actually. Then she took out her biggest canvas because her evening had gone to hell and she was feeling reckless. She tried to conjure up the memory of the red divan so she could recreate it on the canvas, but it kept coming in and out of focus and changing.

She decided not to decide what to paint. She decided she would let herself go, and, as she dipped into random color jars, as she stroked however felt comfortable to her arm, she began to truly relax, and the more that she relaxed, the easier her painting became. It became almost trance-like – as if the picture had already created itself and there was nothing she could do to stop it from coming into existence. She was merely a hand attached directly to the picture, entirely without will.

She painted all night, past when the sun rose, past when her alarm went off for work, past her shift at The Tropical Cove. She used a bright spectrum of colors, some of which she had never opened until that night. And, finally, when she felt she couldn't keep herself awake a second longer, she stood back from the easel and viewed it.

It was a farmhouse – a simple, charming farmhouse. There were crooked little shutters and geese in the front yard and sunflowers as big as watermelons. A woman with an apron and a bonnet that didn't match her dress was standing near a well. A farmer in frayed overalls shaded his eyes from the sun. It was unlike anything she'd painted before.

She stood back from it and thought it was her best work ever. It was so real and at the same time so fantastic. Every detail was perfect and essential, every shape so strong and clean. Sure, it was a painting of a farmhouse, but it captured so much more in mood and message.

And perhaps the most appealing quality of all: It was familiar. She knew it would have the power to conjure up fondness in even the most critical onlooker because it was so familiar. It was like being presented with a picture you had dreamt up a long time ago and then forgotten about. The vulnerable truth of a familiar farmhouse.

A terrible thought struck her then and she gasped. She reached for her purse where it lay on the table. She fiddled with the clasp for what seemed like several minutes; her hand was shaking. At last, she broke it, and the contents of her purse flew out and landed on the table, on the floor, and that goddawful scarf, that tacky Kmart cartoon of a scarf landed in her lap and she saw it. It *was* familiar. She had just painted it.

First, she shredded the scarf. She got out her scissors and cut it and cut it until the pieces were so small that they stuck to the scissors and then she burned them in the ashtray. The painting was next. She slashed it relentlessly with her biggest kitchen knife until she was satisfied that the scene was indistinguishable, and then, utterly exhausted, she dragged it down the block, behind the corner grocery, and hurled it into the dumpster.

Rob called the next day. He said he wanted to "talk things over".

"Alright," she said.

"I don't understand how you became so angry at me. It was only a movie." He sounded like a stranger, so calm and rational. "There are a lot of things that I – "

"I know why," she told him.

"What?" he said.

"I know why I was so angry," she said. "That woman in the movie – she made the wrong choice. She could have gone off with that gallery man-ager, but instead she chose to stay with that creep. Why? So she could watch him play with her cat?"

"What do you mean 'wrong choice'?"

"It's very simple. She chose the wrong man for her."

Rob said, "Maybe she didn't have a choice. Maybe she was in love."

Jeanine said, "Let me tell you something, Rob: People always have a choice."

"Then why am I calling you?" he said.

It was the last thing Rob ever said to her and she tried not to think about it, but it didn't take her long to clean her brushes.

6

Surgery

As a cosmetic surgeon, she took away everyone's most embarrassing and weakest feature. Her hand never failed. People left her office looking normal for the first time in years – or the first time ever. Along with three walls of solid beige, she had a wall of thank-you letters, most with pictures. One of her clients did orange juice commercials now.

She herself was not classically pretty. She could envision a better version of her own face with more prominent cheekbones, a smaller nose, and a smaller forehead (which is what had made Norma Jean into Marilyn). She knew how to do all of it, and she had friends who could do it to her. But there wasn't anything on her face that screamed out "freak." She was average-looking and she was fine with that.

She had just given up coffee yesterday, going on a thousand minutes now, and she sat in the big red leather armchair that her father had donated to her office, surfing the internet for a dress. She had a date next weekend, with a chiropractor, and she wanted something new for it. She wanted to look young and casual and not quite so short, but all of her dresses were holiday dresses. She did a search on the words "sparkle" and "dress" and was presented with a shift made entirely of pale pink sequins and ostrich feathers. Too much, she thought. She wanted to look more normal.

The antique cuckoo clock her father had donated to the office went off and startled her. It was dangerous to be startled during a surgery, so she kept it out in the lobby, but it was so loud that it still startled her in her own office. She seized this opportunity to return to work, shutting down her dress search and opening the folder in front of her.

Every couple years, there was something very unusual – a double earlobe, a missing chunk of cheek – and she never knew when it would come. No matter how detailed the description in the folder, the "before" photos were always a shock to her in these cases. This was one of those. She leaned in and squinted and her adrenaline began to rush in.

It was a stunning woman with a supermodel's face. She had a beautiful body, younger than her years and toned. But on her back, there was a small black-feathered wing. It was placed where an angel's wing might have been placed, but there was only one and it was tiny. Could it move? Could this woman control its movement? She could hardly wait to see it live. How was it connected? She decided to go back to coffee, just until this surgery was done. She needed to be sharp.

The day that the woman came in, she had four cups of coffee and a little weed. She was ready. The woman, whose name was Ingrid, moved like a dancer and wore a big black cape and a patchwork dress and boots. She had hair like Elvira, and she stared for a while before she spoke each time, her big green eyes always hungry for a different answer than the one she was given.

Yes, it would scar. Yes, there would be a co-pay. Yes, it was unlike any surgery she had done up to this point. No, there was no one else who would have this type of experience.

She tried to work in her own questions. Had this been there from birth? Yes, it had. Did it move involuntarily? No, it was under her control. Did it hurt? No, it didn't hurt.

She had her date with the chiropractor that night. She wore a dress from the mall, a dress of which there were ten thousand copies worldwide, a dress she had seen on television. She wanted her personality to stand out more than the dress, but it didn't. He never called.

The woman with the wing came back in for her scheduled surgery a week later. These are the people who hunt me down, she thought, who really need me. He didn't need me, but this beautiful stranger does, this stranger who smells like incense and wears a ring on every finger and can't stop coughing and re-applying her red lipstick. Ingrid.

They always go out so peacefully. They never get all the way to ten when they count. They never stir or have a nightmare during their time out. They go all the way out to someplace they already know, even as she cuts them, even as she drills and saws and tears them to pieces, even as she stiches through their skin.

This wing, though – this wing was connected. At first, it seemed like it was connected only to her spine. But then it seemed to be connected sort of indirectly to her upper arm – and to her heart, her brain, and her lungs. No problem. Anything can be severed if it is done very carefully. The only casualty would be the wing itself. A snip here and snap there. Blood splattered onto her lab coat.

When the wing was fully severed, the woman stopped breathing, her heart stopped beating, and she died. There was this game the surgeon used to play with her little brother where they kept removing parts of their building-block castle until it fell, trying not to remove a piece that would make it topple. She had removed a piece that had toppled this woman's entire existence. The cuckoo clock went off. She walked into the lobby, all business, and tore it down. She threw it into the wastebasket and kicked it across the room. She called her assistant. "Ingrid couldn't tolerate the anesthesia," she said. Then she hung up before saying good-bye and brought the cuckoo clock out to the dumpster. Then she went to the wing itself, picked it up, fondled it a little, and imagined attaching it to her own body, in the exact spot where it had been on Ingrid.

If she did that, though, she would be a freak. She would be a cosmetic surgeon with a small black wing on her back. She would be a first date with a small black wing on her back. She would be alone.

She could never put this wing back and there was no real reason for her to have removed it to begin with, except that it was freakish.

With expert precision, she removed each black feather from the wing, and then, with surgical thread, she stitched them onto her white lab coat. It was the first time she had done any work on herself. None of her patients even cared, because it was up near the collar like she was trying to be fancy, but she knew it was weird and that comforted her.

On her next date, she wore her lab coat with the feathers over her dress. It looked like evening wear. When her date asked her to take the jacket off for dinner, she screamed, "Why?! Why do I have to take it off?! Because it's different?!"

"No," he said, very matter-of-factly. "Because it's ugly."

She soared past him, out the door, into the night, the moonlight hitting her feathers. She ran, but none of the feathers fell off; they were so well-attached to her coat. She was starting to sense air beneath the feathers, air that might lift her up off the ground and really take her somewhere. All the parts she had removed, all the crooked noses, all the sags in the cheeks and the flatness in the chests, she wanted to put them back on the people from whom she had taken them. She sobbed silently and sank back to the ground. That wing had been the essence of Ingrid. Everything had been connected to that wing. Everything had been dependent on it. And she had cut it off.

She screamed out into the parking lot. She tore a feather off her coat and ate it. A stranger brought her into the ladies' room to clean up a little, and she stood there, entirely still, fixated on a hairy mole on her neck that she had never noticed before. She would never forget it again – pudgy round red thing with spikes of dark hair jutting out in all directions. She washed it carefully.

Then she put her feathers back on and soared into fields that haven't been named yet.

7

If Teen Novels Were Real

Even though Riley was a straight woman, she would never forget the first moment that she saw Anastasia. It was in high school, she was late for class, and Anastasia was already writing on the chalkboard. Her short spiky straight hair was not blond but bright gold. Her perfect skin was the whitest that Riley had ever seen and it gleamed, almost as if it would glow in the dark. Anastasia had an oval face with wide-set big black eyes, high jaunty cheekbones, big lips, and a small straight nose. She was not without flaws – she was a bit too tall for a girl, had a faint scar on one cheekbone, and she had a flat chest and big knees that were wider than her legs. These few supposed flaws would last past adolescence and remain there for all of her adult life, but she was somehow so strikingly beautiful, the sunlight hitting her gold hair as it fell over her black bandana, that her flaws only served to make her even more beautiful. You could put someone perfect next to her and she would outshine them. Without moving, without speaking, without posing, she was just incredibly innately striking.

Riley was a creative type, seeing beauty in many strange places, but she was not alone in seeing Anastasia as a great beauty. Later that year, the school hallways would be covered in collages of Anastasia – and she was only a freshman. Any guy from any nearby high school would dump his girlfriend in a heartbeat for a chance with her.

Riley was very pretty in high school, she always had a boyfriend, she was invited to all the best parties and to four different proms, and because she had naturally red, naturally curly hair, her beauty was unique, but she also had the widely-accepted ballet body, a really nice face (for a few years there), and a killer smile. That may be why Anastasia chose her as a friend. But Anastasia's beauty was on a whole different level. She was invited to model for local department stores, to be a free guest at Martha's Vineyard, to be dangled on the arm of the most stunning and sophisticated men of all ages, she was cast without audition, hired on the spot for anything, and everyone in the small city of Portland, Maine had a photograph of her somewhere, if not a stack of photos, because having her in your life somehow made you special and meant that you had made it socially.

That wasn't really what it meant, though, because Anastasia was an extreme hippie and not socially exclusive in any way. She loved the losers and the freaks most of all. Ironically, the losers and the freaks all thought that her befriending them meant that they were now popular, but what it actually meant was that she liked being a star and those were the people who were willing to worship her the most.

She was in the highest academic classes and she was clever in her wry humor, she learned skills quickly, and she employed logic in her life. She excelled at drawing, although she rarely did it, and in choosing clothing for herself. She was extremely friendly. She would meet another best friend every couple days and sometimes add an entire group of teens to her fan club in one night. She was never great at generating ideas – she would hear a new idea, something to do, that seemed fun, that other people were doing, and then she would do that exact thing – but no one cared about this lack of originality. Her beauty was better than watching a movie. It made your life surreal just to have her talk to you.

Over time, Riley did notice other things about her, though. She had a strange conscience. She was not lacking one, but it was not one that you could easily understand. She was a vegetarian from a very young age, although Riley also wondered if it was for vanity's sake and the source of her gleaming skin. But she constantly made out with other people's serious boyfriends, sometimes even sleeping with them, and always ending the relationships that the guys had been in. Some of those relationships had been headed for marriage and none of them were ever restored. For this, she only felt remorse if the girl found out and even then only remorse that she knew. She was constantly trying to outdo other people. If you showed her a piece that you wrote, she would whip up a meaningless page of pretty words and descriptions, read it to you, and insist that your English teacher had told her that she was the best writer in the world. If you were walking downtown with her and one other friend, she would always maneuver until she was in the middle with one person on either side.

There were girls who mocked Anastasia for these types of things. Her beauty had given her so much confidence that she had become a bit unaware. She didn't know that she was terrible on the dance floor, that she had no ear for music and that when she sang she looked like she was concentrating very hard for minimal results, that she wasn't gifted at theater, that the story she had been repeating to everyone about a sitcom turning her down because she was "too good" sounded to everyone else like adults trying to spare children's feelings. She had become – or was always – extremely conceited. She would come over with a stack of pictures to show Riley and they would all be of her and only her.

Maybe the conceit was normal for a teen that beautiful, but she also developed really stupid goals. While others were chasing down schools, creating portfolios, planning to have families, putting out albums, or just plain getting really good at something or really knowledgeable about something, she was making up itty-bitty contests in her head – which were visible to other people – and winning them. If the waiter winked once at Riley, she would make him wink twice at her. If a teacher said Riley's history report was brilliant, she would get that same teacher to say something nice about a report that she had already written. If Riley threw two parties that week, she would throw three. You were supposed to notice, I guess, and think that she was superior in all ways.

One of the strangest things about her beauty was how much it fooled people. Riley could remember a fairly intelligent guy that she liked, who had never talked to Anastasia, telling her that Anastasia was beautiful but that it wasn't just what she looked like. What he meant was what everyone believed back then. They weren't shallow – they were drawn to Anastasia because she possessed a deep magic that made her appear beautiful.

Anastasia didn't go to college – even later on, when she would become enraged if you knew something that she didn't or could discuss something that she couldn't. But she moved around the country with various boyfriends and half-assed art projects and waitressing jobs until she finally settled in Maine again and became a social leader of their hippie scene. Her uncle had been part of the underground counterculture, not for anything he made or did, but because he talked about revolution and went to all the right parties. He had played the triangle ironically, which she thought was funny, so she followed his example. She brought her triangle to jams and open mics and she invited all the halfway-good musicians to her house parties so she could play her triangle with them. She dated some of them. She had band after band where she played the triangle. They each had one gig in every amateur venue available and then no more. She put on elaborate costumes and brought her triangle to block parties and parades. The children there loved her, purely for her looks, and all her hundreds of friends thought she was an icon. They wanted to marry her, be her, or learn how to be cool from her. They had been outcast in high school and were trying desperately to live out what they had missed in their teen years now, as adults. She had learned how to act cool by now and they all thought that she was. She let everything go, had no public emotions except joy, didn't believe that anything was wrong except judgment itself, and she always knew where the next great party was. She never got too high or too drunk, she never got attached, and she was still incredibly beautiful, in her sloppy thrift shop clothing. When her cousin from New York City moved to town, all her friends said that even though her cousin was more beautiful, Anastasia had more personality. She thought the same thing. She outright said to Riley once, "I think, with me, it's not just beauty. It's something else." It sounds like it was part of a bigger conversation, but it wasn't. It was just something that she came out and told Riley out of nowhere.

Over time, the pictures of Anastasia became ones of her caught glaring at voluptuous belly dancers. She lost her serious boyfriend to an opera singer. They were all still friends afterward, because that is the cool way to be. She inherited money from her grandmother and traveled Europe a bit. Social media had become big and she documented every step of replacing her boyfriend with a new French one who also played the triangle. Real musicians began posting old photos of her instead of more recent ones. She began taking them down.

She threw herself into her political passions. She had no understanding of what organizations were already doing and how. She created her own club to collect money for coronavirus research. She didn't have enough basic science to know that a Wi-Fi connection could not cause cancer, and she didn't understand why no one signed her door-to-door petition about it. She was losing in faith in the world. Cashiers no longer fell in love with her. No one showed up to help her and her replacement boyfriend to fix their driveway, even after she had told them that she had made free jewelry for everyone. People began sending her clips of local music that was actually good. She would run into women who had been medium-pretty in high school and were now gorgeous.

Anastasia looked cute now. She was certainly not a dog. In the right light and from the right angle, you could see what she had once been. Years of cigarettes and no exercise had taken their toll, though. She was wrinkly and anorexic-looking. She had never learned about makeup and, even with natural non-carcinogenic products being widely available, she was too proud to use it. She began making screwed-up faces when she was photographed. She didn't want anyone to think that this was what she actually looked like.

Where were all the jams and the parties? Everyone had families and careers now. She blamed this on "society". She was not a part of "society". Her old friends tried to be kind, but there wasn't really much for her to do anymore. Suddenly, no one wanted her in their band. Suddenly, she had to make sure that the relationship that she was already in worked out. Suddenly, the photos that were circulating all had other gorgeous women in them. She became very depressed.

At this point, Riley had known many other beautiful women – as beautiful as Anastasia or more so – who had done amazing things in this world and whose internal gifts far outweighed their beauty, but as Anastasia aged, it was not only she who felt disillusioned and confused. Everyone who had known her felt duped. She had captured their attention and brought them on a journey that had led nowhere. They had all thought they were in an 80s movie and that it would end in a big happy party in a mansion by the sea.

From her end, though, she had watched them seek her out, choose her, put her into any job or romance she wanted, tell her that she was talented, she was compassionate, she was fun, and then – in an instant – all of them had turned away, to other fantasies, other distractions. She had merely followed the path that they had laid out for her. And it had brought her to a place where she had lived a long, long time, yet hadn't really lived at all yet.

So one day in her fifties, Anastasia was in her group therapy session, with a man she had cheated with decades ago but no longer remembered, and with Riley, who had only agreed to come as a favor, and Anastasia was trying to have the biggest, most dramatic problem of the group and to describe it in ways that let everyone know that she was a poetic genius. "I feel like I am on a surface ten times more slippery than ice," she said. "People just don't care about anything in this crazy society. They are pretending that it is the product and not the process. It is not what the music sounds like that is important." She made a great flourishing hand gesture as she spoke. Fortunately, she had finally begun wearing deodorant in recent years.

The man she had cheated with flashed back to how she had never moved her hips at all during sex and then to the French girl he had lost because of her. Riley looked at her cell phone to see the time and the facilitator glared at her and asked her to turn it off. A punk rock teenager sneered at all of them and gave up his turn, so Anastasia talked more.

"I am trying to do something with my triangle from the Baroque period, but folks are intimidated by it. There is a funny little man in East Pittston –" She laughed out loud at him and not because he wasn't there, then continued, "who will do it with me. He plays the kazoo. I am making a special soup out of melons for him." She made a haughty self-conscious sniffing sound with her nose, which she did often while speaking.

"Well, that's very nice," the facilitator said.

"Who is that?" asked Riley.

"Soup with melons?!" The punk continued sneering.

"That whole share seemed very pretentious!" the man she had cheated with yelled out in a sudden tantrum.

Anastasia steeled her eyes, but later she cried over that comment as she drove home to her replacement boyfriend.

It was almost as if now that her extreme beauty had faded into a more common one, people could actually see her.

At home were a pile of cheap triangles that were her real therapy, some ugly décor, and Him with his self-obsessed immature laziness, if he was even home. There was a bottle of wine and a stack of old pictures. She had saved them to show to her grandchildren, but she had no grand-children. Sometimes, she showed them to Him, but he just laughed. "You were a totally different person back then," he would say. But that's the thing – she really wasn't a totally different person back then.

If she steered into a tree doing sixty, everyone would think it was an accident, right?

8

Not Your Fight

You watch a stranger play guitar and sing on your street corner to absolutely no audience, and *you* can't even hear any of it yet, because you are still inside, near your window. When he finishes singing, he says something – it looks like the word "Yay" but a sarcastic "Yay" – and then he stands up and suddenly, he is being attacked on the sidewalk by something that you can't see. He still has his guitar in one hand, but he's being beaten up by an invisible enemy.

You can see that it just tore out some of his hair, knocked out a couple of his teeth, and then kneed him really hard in the crotch, but you can't see anything there, except for the man you like. The man rips the invisible thing off of him. When he does, you can tell that it had its claws pressed into his veins, because the inner elbows of both his sleeves have tiny spots of blood on them now. You can see the man try to block it from glomming on to him again, and that he's trying to block it from different angles. Then he's trying to beat it down with his guitar. You can see that the man is wrestling it now, and even that he is winning. You can see that he just pushed it to the ground, but that it grabbed him around the knees and is trying to pull him down like that. You can see that it punched him in the guts and he is doubled-over, vomiting.

But you still can't see anything besides the man himself – you can only see what happens to him and what he does about it. You understand, though, that just because you can't see what he's fighting doesn't mean it isn't real.

You are standing behind your living room window and are not even supposed to be watching it, because it's not your fight, because you can't even perceive what he's fighting, and because it will likely be a long fight. But he stops fighting for a moment and, from a hundred feet away, he looks right at you through your window and smiles at you and it electrocutes you a little and you immediately smile back. You want to go out there just to be a little closer to whatever he is doing. He's sexy and bizarre and you feel like he is haunting your window. From behind your insulated walls and your soundproof window, you start to flinch whenever he gets hit. You can see that he feels everything very deeply, but that he will keep getting up anyway, and sometime in the last few minutes, whatever is happening out there that you *can't* see has somehow become slightly more important than the luxurious nothingness that is happening in your own apartment and its safe, empty silence.

But it doesn't matter what you feel right now – you can't go out there because you can sense that he already likes you, too, and if you go out there right now, that would distract him from what he's doing and then he'd lose. And you can't scream anything out either, because he can't hear you from inside your cozy little apartment, and even if he could, you have nothing useful to say. You don't *know* anything. You try to remind yourself how little you actually know about his fight.

You shut your blinds. You surf the internet, you listen to some music, you cook a stir-fry. You sit down and move the stir-fry around in different patterns without eating it.

You believe that at any second, he might win. Then you could go out there with him and he would play the guitar and you could dance to his music. You think he probably *will* win. You think you can sense it. But you can't tell how long it will take. You open up your blinds again and look out there and he's still fighting. And he looks like he has more energy than before. Still, you can't see what he's up against, and you don't know what it can and can't do to him.

You think it's honorable that he's handling it, though. You think it's romantic that he's handling it. You move your armchair right up near the glass. After a while, squinting from your armchair, with your un-eaten stir-fry still in your lap, you even think you might finally know what it is that he's fighting. You get a picture of the invisible enemy in your head and now it seems so obvious – *so* obvious that you think that he must have thought that you could see this thing clearly when he smiled at you. Maybe that's why he smiled at you. He thought that you could both see this thing.

You want to open up your window and yell out that you have just figured everything out just now. But you can't do that, either, because then he will be forced to yell back in response during his fight, and he could get completely knocked out in that one second. Plus you still can't technically see the enemy – so technically, you are still just *imagining* it. You grab a pen and try to sketch the invisible thing on your dinner napkin, to make it tangible. At first, you are just scribbling according to how you think it moves in negative space. But then when you are finished, you look at the picture and you definitely recognize it. You know this enemy. This enemy has obliterated some of your friends.

Just then, the man rolls out of the field of vision that your window allows, and you can't see him anymore. You grab your napkin drawing, stuff it in your pocket, and run out your door, down the hallway stairs, out the main entrance, and jump the outside steps. But when you get to the sidewalk, there he is, walking away slowly, with his guitar in his hand, like nothing ever happened. You study him for any tiny sign of panic, because you know that *he* can see if the enemy is still there, even if you can't. But he seems completely at peace.

You reach into your pocket and you whip out your napkin drawing. You hold your napkin drawing up against the sky and study it for reference. Your eyes dart around your sketch. You see the motion streaks that you drew on it, and you remember that the enemy could creep out from a hiding spot and attack him from behind at any time, while he is just innocently trying to get home with his guitar. He is just right there, out in the open – and the enemy couldn't have gone that far. You can see that he's walking close to the soft grass at the edge of the sidewalk. So to keep him safe and invisible from the enemy, you quickly and quietly run after him and you jump on his back and try to tackle him from behind, so that he will have to fall flat on the grass behind some bushes.

It doesn't really work, though, because you're so much smaller than he is, and because you have never actually tackled anyone before so you guess you did it wrong. So now he just sort of *has* you on his back and he doesn't fall to the ground. He doesn't even flinch. He doesn't even turn his head to confirm that it's you. He just bends forward a little so you won't fall, and he is still completely at peace.

And then you realize that he has won his fight already, and that you are just some crazy person on his back, riding him down the street, with some made-up theory on a napkin. He seems to take it in stride, though. He keeps walking down the block, at an even pace, with you on his back. Then he starts whistling. It's this strange, clear whistling that is masculine and high at the same, and his whistling goes through your entire body in a wave of tiny vibrations, as if you are an instrument. He spins you around on his back for a while, like your dad used to do when you were little. Then he walks you over to the door that you ran out from and slides you off his back. And then he stands completely still, like a trained animal, while he tries to figure out if you want him to touch you yet. But he can sense that you have something you need to do first, so he just hangs out and watches as you rip up your ridiculous napkin drawing.

His eyes rest on your fingers as you rip. Suddenly, you wonder if he can actually see your napkin drawing – or if he can only see your fingers ripping up something invisible.

9

Behind Tall Hedges

His mother was always easy to spot in the train station. She was six feet tall and bought her trench coats in bright pastels, no matter what the season. She towered like a long, slim Crayola crayon in a box of neutral and black-clad New Yorkers, like an innocent little girl dressed up for her birthday party, yet somehow everyone else around her was draped in ethnic print fabrics or wearing studded leather pants with their big sprayed-up hair or army jackets or bondage wear. If you couldn't see her face, she seemed lost – kind, even – but as soon as her face was in view, you could see her thick, leather-y skin and the focused cruelty in her tiny blue eyes. It was the reason only the people behind her stood close to her. To them, she was still a pastel crayon – whimsical and sweet. In front of her and to her sides, however, there were little clearings in the crowd, places where no one wanted to stand. She put her vein-y, gnarled, little claw up to her flat gray hair to flatten it perfectly, and then clutched both hands around her straw purse, digging her yellow fingernails into it as far as they would go.

Declan watched her from the train window, writing out her description in his battered leather journal. It had dragons embossed on both covers and had been a gift from Grandma Rose. It was his favorite possession. *"Her wrath goes before her"* he wrote, *"but leaves no trail."*

Then he wrapped his journal up in a plaid flannel that had body odor on it and shoved it into his nearly-matching battered leather backpack. He had no suitcase, since he still kept a closet at home. He sat at the window until the last possible minute, watching, and was the last one off the train.

She smiled at him, a thin creepy smile that disappeared quickly, hugged him because that was what you did when your son came home broke, and looked him over, inch by inch. He looked like a nerdy bum to her, like someone who slept on park benches but somehow had access to a Dungeons and Dragons game during the day. She kissed him on the head and he recoiled. She smelled like that familiar smell of baby powder, Woolite, cinnamon Trident, and cigarettes – with just a hint of scotch.

Together, they shoved through the crowd and out to the line of midnight taxis.

"How was the train ride?" she asked him.

"It was smooth," he answered. "Smooth and fast. I had a ham sandwich in the dining car. Then I napped."

They climbed into the first cab together.

"Do you want to put that in the trunk?" She asked, pointing to his backpack. "There will be more space." She grabbed it from him and climbed out.

From behind the open trunk door, she unlatched his backpack, reached inside, felt his journal wrapped inside his flannel, grabbed it, and placed the journal into her purse. Then she re-latched both bags quickly, threw the backpack into the trunk, and slammed the trunk door. When she looked up, she realized that the cab driver stood at her side, ready to offer her assistance. Unsure of what the driver had seen, she stared him down and took her place in the back of his cab again.

"You look as though you lost weight," she said to her son.

"I haven't. You look wonderful yourself. Is that trench coat new?"

"Yes, it was a gift from your Grandma Rose."

"How is Grandma Rose doing?"

He was looking out the window at the skyline, wondering why Grandma Rose always looked younger than his mother somehow.

"As well as can be expected for someone in her eighties, I suppose."

He was supposed to have gotten the door for his mother and to have taken care of his own backpack. He would do better at the other end of the ride. Millions of pedestrians wove in between the traffic. His eyes scanned the sidewalks. He had forgotten how many manholes there were here. The purple-black sky had disappeared behind the buildings and in the enclosed space of that backseat, the familiar smell of her became nauseating and he cracked his window.

He stared at his own reflection in the protective plastic shield between them and the driver. With his conservatively-cut dark hair and tiny blue eyes, his fair skin with faded freckles, his baggy gray cable-knit sweater and serious intent, he was the portrait of a brooding Irishman. He wished he had bought a newspaper at the station. There were several stories he was following very closely and he didn't think the internet would do them justice.

Later, his mother would tuck him into his old bed, beneath the blue quilt that Grandma Rose had made him. She would mumble all the usual prayers, draw the shade to make the room pitch black, and kiss him again on the top of his head. Then she would go into the living room, a dozen different-sized Madonna statues staring back at her with a small broken television in the middle of them. It only got one channel. She would turn on the news at a ridiculously high volume, then sit down in her armchair and light a cigarette, and only after she could lower the volume and hear him snoring softly, would she open up that journal.

When she finally did, it was close to sunrise. There was a newspaper clipping right in the front of it. Some tiny country in Africa was under attack. She didn't bother with that. The handwritten sentences were about her – she knew they would be.

When people tell me I have her eyes, I hope they do not mean that I have that cruel expression and I hope they do not mean that I could ever see the world the way that she sees the world – in black and white. What color is blood in a black and white world?

Grandma Rose said to know and to always be on guard. I can never shut my mind off because I live in the midst of evil. She and I both know that the evil is her daughter and my mother, and that we will always be too moral or too weak to fully escape. We both avoid looking at her as we pass the Thanksgiving turkey. Her words seem to splatter everything with a disfiguring acid, everything she sees gets splattered with it, and we are all forced to watch it dissolve from its original form into a new ugliness she has created. My father, New York, the ingredients in bread – nothing is left untouched by her.

Grandma Rose could not be more different. She is a light that gets into every dark crevice that you show her and warms it and brightens it until you almost feel healed and whole again. Her radiance is tangible. From her rocking chair straight into my heart – an energy with which to face the world. She sees me. She tells me stories. She is without that creepy vengeance that cannot see itself but can only see a world worth punishing.

Another newspaper clipping – this one a photo of a fierce tribal leader defending his small country – and another photo – also black and white – of the invaders, smug in their tanks, barely visible.

I asked to see Grandma Rose's journal. I feel like if there is anyone still living whom she would show that to, it would be me, but she told me ... possibly the worst thing I know about Mother now. She said that Mother stole her journal.

At first, I thought she must be mistaken, but the more I thought about it, the more I realized that my mother would have stolen Grandma Rose's journal, read it, and kept it. She enjoys power over others – and not the kind of power that is willingly given.

I think Grandma Rose saw my anguish when she told me that. She said that Mother has her own way of being good in the world. She tutors orphans. She really cares about those orphans. She teaches them to read and to write and they go on to have very different lives than they might have had.

Then Grandma Rose got up – she never gets up – and she got real close to me – and she said, "You will be asked to keep many secrets about your parents. You will be asked to keep the secrets of what they are really like and what they have done wrong, and you will be mostly asked to keep it secret from your parents themselves."

There was another clipping of that country after they had lost, its once-barren streets were filled with fruit vendors and the enemy's flag was flying proudly in the background.

"Her wrath goes before her but leaves no trail."

She slammed the journal shut and dug her yellow nails into its soft leather. Very carefully, she stood up on her armchair, still in her pastel trench coat so as not to waste money on heat, and reached behind the grandfather clock and into a hole in its back. She felt around for the cold plastic cover of her mother's journal and when she felt it, she slid her son's journal right above it.

He woke up to the sound of traffic, but not because the sound of traffic had just begun. He lit a cigarette and sat on the windowsill. He turned on news radio. He tried to smoke and listen and look into the neighbor's window, but instead he imagined falling out of the window, then having to jump out of the window to escape a fire, then being shot through the window. He began sweating and shaking slightly. He got up and got dressed. Then he took that outfit off because he was afraid it looked improper, and then he got dressed again. He reached for his journal and it wasn't there. He gasped and trembled. Then he immediately rejected the moment from his memory. He smoked another cigarette, this one stolen deftly from his mother's pack, and shaved and left while Mother was still asleep in her armchair.

The elevator took a long time coming. He worried that it was defective. When it came, he leaned into it and tried to read the date on the last inspection license before he stepped into it. When it closed, he pressed for the ground floor three times, even though it had lit up the first time, and then he pressed his fingertips into his jeans until even his short perfect fingernails dug into his thighs. The elevator ding-ed at the floor so suddenly that it startled him and he jumped slightly. Then he pulled down the sunglasses from his head and walked out into the world.

He passed a group of young girls who he thought were improperly dressed. They smiled at him, but he pretended not to see them. He passed a homeless man who smelled slightly of scotch and pretended not to see him, either. He said a quick prayer in his head that he would never degenerate so far as to lose all self-control. He stopped noticing who he was passing and turned into a bakery. He thought about getting some pastry, but worried it would cause him to get blemishes from the sugar. He didn't know all the ingredients that they used. The foreigner in the corner looked dangerous. He turned and left. He walked further and turned into a Chinese Restaurant. He tried to look tough. He looked everyone in the face with his tough look, but then he noticed a stray cat running around and being shooed out. That's a sure sign of diseases, he thought, and he left there, too.

He stopped at a street vendor and bought a newspaper. You are supposed to bring flowers when you come home and he had failed at buying flowers last night to meet his mother, so he bought some flowers, too.

"What kind would you like?" the vendor asked him.

"The kind for coming home, for my mother," he answered, and wound up with trendy pink peonies; the vendor had bought too many of them.

"This isn't what I meant," he said.

The vendor glared at him. He thought the vendor might say something cruel to him, so he said, "Never mind – these are fine" and he left.

He thought that he saw roaches at the grocer, when he was buying bread and ham and milk, but he went ahead and bought them, anyway. I hope these are alright, he thought, and started on his way home.

He felt on the verge of remembering something important when a punk with a chain approached him and swung the chain near his head. He neither flinched nor stepped back nor screamed, nor did he swing back. He stood limply, staring into the punk's eyes with a vacant sincerity. The punk was freaked out and left, and Declan continued his way home.

Their building had a tall hedge around it, which was unusual for the city. It seemed much more like something you would see in the suburbs. It concealed a thin strip of grass, which he used to play in as a boy. He stood staring at it. It was terrible grass, all patchy and brown. He remembered taking his pet turtle Netflix out here to play; he remembered when his now off-and-on girlfriend Mary was just that little redhead girl from Apartment Four, and when she had shoved him down to the ground and kissed him; he remembered burying a sack of pennies and making a treasure map to it and leaving it in the laundry room, so that anyone who found it could excitedly dig it up. He laughed. He tried to keep laughing and keep moving, but then the memories of her came back too fast for him to stop them.

She was crouched down at his level, back when her hair was still a dark brown. She was wearing plaid shorts that went all the way down past her knees. She was crouching so that no one else would hear her hissing her words at him. "No one else gets this dirty when they play outside. There is something really wrong with you. You are going to grow up to be incompetent. You seem to have a warped mind. I'd rather see you dead than see you grow up to have the kind of life you are going to have." She grabbed the ice cream cone out of his hands and threw it in the hedge.

He tried to fight back the tears the entire time she was saying these things to him. They are only words, he told himself, but he finally broke down crying, his little body curled up on the patchy brown lawn. When he finally looked back up at her, she had a sick little smile on her face.

His teachers at boarding school, the ones who liked him anyway, used to wonder why he had stayed in contact with her long after he was old enough to legally cut it off. He never really could explain that to them.

She wrote him love letters – personal ones. She did all the right Mom stuff with him – museums and catch and mending his socks. They did crafts and saw Ice Capades and Barnum and Bailey Circus and went to see Grandma Rose. Mother seemed to make the most effort of everyone that he knew, and she also seemed the most concerned with his day-to-day well-being. While Grandma Rose was bent on him developing creatively and having enough freedom, Mother noticed the nuts and bolts of what he needed: a math tutor, more iron in his diet, to avoid that heavy-metal chick. She cooked three square meals a day for him whenever he was home, all the way into adulthood. She was the one who taught him to tell time, to tie his shoelaces, the capital of every state, and the times tables. Actually, she's the one who taught him to read, long before pre-school. She used to read him stories in his crib. Eventually, he learned the stories by listening, and then she would make up fake endings to entertain herself and he would yell out, "No! That's not how it ends!" So then she taught him the alphabet. It was between that and buying a bunch of new books, probably. When he was four, he could read to himself. Mother loved that. His pre-school teacher hated it because when she would read a story to class, he would get bored and start reading his own book. She didn't believe that he really understood it. Grandma Rose would get on the phone with his teacher and, with her low cool voice, big sunglasses, and attitude, would set that teacher straight. Grandma Rose believed it was because he was a genius, way more advanced than the other children. But really, it was simply that Mother had taught him to read at a very young age and she had taught him very thoroughly. Teaching was what she did best.

If Mother had not won custody of him, he would have turned out a little dumber, no question there.

She would go years without making him cry. Well, years might be an exaggeration – she would go months without making him cry sometimes. Then her eyes would change and she would tell him that his father didn't really love him, that he ruined everything, that her students made fun of his face when he wasn't there, that he couldn't keep a secret, that he needed to learn how to do more things he didn't like, that he didn't run fast enough. She would scream at him in the park. He was tiny; his legs were only tiny. That was as fast as he could go. Sometimes, many many times, he would burst into tears. Whenever he did, she would get that sick little smile. Over time, he figured out that if he could manage to not cry, she wouldn't smile, but either way, it always felt the same. He wanted to be able to leave when she did that, but he couldn't get to Grandma Rose's by himself yet.

And then her eyes would change back. She would tell him that he was the most handsome boy in the world, that his skin felt like velvet, that it was amazing that he had turned out so well, and that she thought that he took after Grandma Rose. She sometimes seemed to admire Grandma Rose as much as he did. Except when she said mean things about her weight and how she spent all her father's money and ran his estate into the ground.

Other times, she would list off all the ways Grandma Rose had failed him as a grandparent. She claimed that in Grandma Rose's senior housing apartment, there were roaches crawling across him while he slept, because she was so dirty and negligent. She claimed that Grandma Rose had said that since hadn't gotten custody of him, she would kill herself. He was seven still. When she dropped him off at senior housing for a visit, he asked Grandma Rose what happened to people who killed themselves. He had always believed in the concept of souls and needed to know what would happen to them. Grandma Rose mistakenly thought he was suicidal himself – at age seven. This was before the days when shrinks were acceptable for kids. If he went to a shrink, that would mean he was asylum-level crazy. For weeks, Grandma Rose told him how people who killed themselves were always known to regret it at the last minute and try to fight to survive. She said you never knew what was going to happen next in life and you wanted to stick around to see. At the end of those weeks, they were each convinced that the other one wouldn't kill themselves and they both rested easy.

Grandma Rose loved stories – telling them, hearing them, reading them, and writing them. She loved the moment when Declan couldn't wait to hear what was coming next. She would pause and take a sip of her tea, smiling up at him while he waited. She loved it when he asked questions about her characters. And she loved to think about *his* stories while she was holed up in senior housing and would often cut her floor's Bingo game to daydream about the stories he had told her. Some of them were true about his adventures at college, and some of them were strange tales about dragons interacting with people.

He had bought her a new journal. It was good for her arthritis to write things down. After she wrote a new story, the pain in one hand would subside, at least, for a few hours. She had a new story about herself playing crazy pranks on all the nurses there. She couldn't wait to show it to him.

He was supposed to stop by around six that evening, but he was at home and thinking of whipping out his own journal when his off-and-on girlfriend, Mary, called.

Mary came over because Mother was still out tutoring orphans. She lay down on the floor of his bedroom in her woven poncho and high brown boots and she played with her long red hair and claimed she wanted to get out of New York forever. He knew she had no money. He offered to tell her a story.

Mary, despite not being named Moira, was Irish-American and real into her roots, so he asked her if she had heard the old Irish legend of The Hedgemasters. She shook her long hair that she hadn't.

He thought about spreading out on the floor next to her, but was too afraid. He told her with a crooked grin that he couldn't believe she hadn't heard this yet. He pretended it was a huge hole in her education that must be remedied immediately. Finally, he sat down across the floor from her and leaned against his wall.

You see, England tried to starve Ireland. Obviously, they don't mention that in their history books, but they wanted slave labor and more land and they poisoned the crops (unable to reach the potatoes underground, which is why the population didn't completely die off.) They also destroyed all the libraries. They also made it illegal upon penalty of death for the Irish to teach their children to read. It was the moment in Irish history where they might have become a Third World country, had they not taken history into their own hands.

They held secret meetings. They figured out that, because they had these very tall hedges separating one neighbor's fields from another's that they could use these hedges to hide behind. They asked for volunteers who were not only the best teachers, but who would risk their lives, to come to each village dressed as yardsmen with a whole variety of hedge clippers. The children (who would have no books or notebooks with them, lest their parents should be hung) would gradually convene behind a hedge that was being trimmed.

Needless to say, there was no goofing off in these classes. Imagine if you knew that your teacher could be hung for teaching you each lesson. Everyone's homework was always done. And some of the Hedgemasters were caught. And they were hung. And then more volunteers would come forward. In Ireland, they still know the names of all of these teachers, the ones who survived and the ones who were killed.

Several generations of Irish grew up. Some of them were named James Joyce, Oscar Wilde, Jonathon Swift, and George Bernard Shaw. Some families left for America, due to limited potatoes. The O'Connors, who would raise Flannery O'Connor, and the McCourts, who would raise Frank McCourt, were on those boats.

They were great writers. But The Hedgemasters were the heroes.

His mother's Irish-American. Funny that Declan would know a legend that pays homage to her, isn't it? Well, he would tell a legend about a sadist instead, but they don't have legends about that.

He didn't learn The Hedgemaster story from her, though. He read it on his own. But he thinks about it sometimes when he pictures Mother walking up flight after flight of tenement stairs to drill the orphans in their lessons. Some of them grow up to be teachers. A lot of them will probably be at her funeral someday.

10

Best in Honor

After only three days in jail without her special conditioner, Kim's long curly red hair was beginning to dreadlock. The reality of being temporarily trapped had set in yesterday, and now it was just a matter of daydreaming until her arraignment hearing. She had one more hour. She stretched out in her bedding on the concrete floor. A guard popped in and threw bologna sandwiches wrapped in Saran Wrap at everyone. There were seven other women being held in her cell (although they weren't the same seven as when she had arrived), plus a sink, a toilet, and a television mounted in a corner of the ceiling.

The television was covered by a plastic shield and there was no remote for it. Kim didn't own a television at home and to her, the loud unceasing sitcoms and infomercials were the worst part of being in jail. Everything else about it was rough or uncomfortable, but that television was outright invasive. Everything else about it was just part of another wild adventure, a part that she would tell her friends about later – but that hour-long commercial for a treadmill, that was a suburban imposition. She didn't want to hear it.

And she only *did* hear it for first ten or twelve hours. Now it was just white noise, like a nearby ocean or Manhattan traffic or crickets. The rerun of *Roseanne* that was playing had become her new silence.

The cop had paused for long periods of time between each section of her intake interview. He had paused to look her over in her designer dress that she had bought secondhand and added different sleeves to. He had paused to consider that someone who had gone to school where she had gone to school, and now worked where she worked, was getting booked for violence. And he had paused to check in privately with the officer who had arrested her.

"Do you have any tattoos?" he had asked her.

"No," she had said. "There isn't really a particular symbol that I gravitate toward over a long time period," she had added, as if this were a social conversation and he was simply getting to know her better as a person.

"Do you have any history of addiction issues?"

"No. Except soda. There aren't any groups for soda recovery, though."

He had squinted at her, trying to discern if she was joking or mentally unstable. "Do you feel that there should be a group for that?" he had asked her.

"Absolutely," she had answered. "That way, we could chip in for other refreshments – to go with all the soda." She hadn't smiled.

"Do you ever feel someone's watching you?" he had asked her.

"Yes," she had answered.

"When do you feel that way?" he had pressed on, feeling like now he was really getting somewhere.

"When someone's actually watching me."

He had laughed.

"You have no record at all," he had informed her.

"I certainly hope not," she had said. "Will I have one now?"

He had shuffled some papers around and looked her in the eye. "Probably not."

Then she had put everything into a clear plastic bag with her inmate number on it – her dress, her shoes, her watch, her purse; had changed into scrubs and slipper-socks; and had used her one call to ask her roommate to call out of work for her for the next two days – she didn't want it to come from this number. She had spent her first few hours in the cell asking everyone what they were in for and listening to their stories. Some of them had talked for hours about a prescription they had forged. Others had talked very little about approaching their exes with various weapons. One kept telling different stories about her crime, changing it entirely every ten minutes or so and interrupting whoever was talking to chime in with her latest version. She was Kim's favorite – Lydia. That lady hadn't been talking to confess or to sate anyone's curiosity – she had been talking about it purely to have fun and to be entertaining. Just before she had been released to her daughter's custody, Lydia had evolved the story to being a pirate who had sailed along the coast of Oregon stealing chocolate.

After Lydia had left, Kim had started exercising. She had done calisthenics, yoga, and ballet barre. Sometimes, other inmates had joined her, sometimes not. She had been woken up in the middle of the night to go to the office and to take her mug shot and she had smiled for it. When they had brought her back, she had watched a really young inmate try to seduce a guard through their bars. When that had stopped being interesting, she had gone back to sleep.

The next morning, the inmates had told Kim that she was the only one who had slept. In an effort to sleep well themselves, more of them had begun joining in Kim's spontaneous and frequent exercise sessions throughout her second day, solemnly following the careful technique and routine that she had laid out for them.

On her third morning, everyone but Kim herself had woken up sore. It is easy to deal with muscle soreness in jail, though. You simply sit still all day and stare at that plastic-covered screen. Eventually, a warden will slide the door open and throw more food at you.

***

It all started three months ago, when Kim's cousin Carol took a public bus for the first time in her life.

Carol was the type of woman who would not leave the house until every hair was in place and her socks matched her sweater and her eyebrows looked like twisted ribbons. She was the type of woman who clipped coupons, who brushed her dog's teeth, and who had lived in the same town all her life, wondering why Mr. Right had always married someone else and left her alone to alphabetize her spice rack.

Fortunately, she was also beautiful. Her bone structure and her skin were perfect, she was in excellent shape, and she had the most popular type of beauty: blond hair and blue eyes – which is *why* Mr. Right would always begin dating her to begin with, long before he received a stack of index cards from her that listed off different possible outfits from his closet. "Just for reference," she would whisper.

Carol never took the bus. She took her Range Rover. But today, it was in the shop, and taxis were slow, and she wanted to get to the bookstore to meet that cookbook author that she liked. It is likely that if all these circumstances had not occurred in conjunction with each other, she and Josh would never have been in the same place at any point in their entire lives.

"It was the strongest chemistry I have ever felt!" she told Kim later on the phone.

Josh, apparently, was rugged and earthy. He had warm, sweet brown eyes and he was toned and muscular. He had charisma and courage. He had adventures and his own set of ethics. Josh was too intelligent to be society's pawn and too wise to waste time on any conventional successes. He had a huge, unprotected heart and no responsibilities whatsoever.

In short, Josh was a bum. This was evident to the rest of the bus by his extremely tattered clothing and his frequent naps on the bus, but Carol was mesmerized by his longing for her. Josh hadn't talked to a woman who had smelled good for a while, so he really pulled out all the stops, even reading her palm for free.

Carol missed her stop.

***

Two weeks later, Kim was at Carol's house to help her set up a dinner party for a colleague's promotion. Josh was there, in the suit Carol had bought him, and he was telling Carol that she looked ugly and Carol was crying.

"Carol is beautiful! You are crazy!" Kim yelled at him.

"Kim, Josh has been through a lot – you have no idea what he has been through – and he has been living on the streets. It is very insensitive of you to be raising your voice at him."

Carol and Josh hugged each other. Then they kissed. Then they went into her bedroom for an hour.

Kim set up the dinner party by herself. When they came out from the bedroom, Josh immediately told Carol that she was stupid.

***

The next week, Josh took all of Carol's vintage records and sold them to a consignment store.

Carol called Kim crying and talked for an hour about how it was going to break his heart when she told him it was over.

Kim told her that she wasn't too concerned with Josh's heart, and Carol told her that was insensitive.

***

The next week, Carol called to say that she and Josh were now engaged to be married, but Carol was looking for a new job because Josh had screamed in her supervisor's face at the dinner party. Her voice sounded clear and happy and excited about her future.

Kim was silent.

***

The next week, Carol called up absolutely hysterical that her dog was missing. A couple days later, Josh told her that he had given her dog to another homeless man, so that he would get better donations from the public.

In the most sensitive tone she could manage, Kim said, "Do you think you might be rushing into this marriage too quickly, Carol? Don't you want to sit back and just enjoy dating for a while first?"

"This isn't just some fling, Kim. This is serious. I love Josh."

***

The next week, Josh went to the emergency room after Carol threw a wineglass at his head and hit it.

Carol paid for the visit.

Josh slept outside for the night as further punishment for whatever he had done.

Carol called Kim and talked for hours about how this relationship was sick and must be filling a deep psychological need rooted in her childhood.

Kim agreed.

The next day, Carol let Josh back inside and they made love and went back to planning their wedding.

***

The next week, Kim went on a date with a professional soccer player from Chile. He talked about his country, about living here in America, about Chilean literature and Chilean theater and how Chilean women dress.

Meanwhile, Kim talked about Carol, Josh, and Carol and Josh.

Their evening ended early.

Kim went home and wrote the perfect speech to give to Carol to talk her out of this insanity.

***

Carol came over, crying, a few weeks later, in the middle of the night.

Josh had set all of her photo albums on fire and then put the fire out by peeing on them. Kim decided it was the right moment for her perfect speech. She delivered it with great conviction and Carol listened to all of it with rapt attention. Then Carol went to sleep and Kim stayed up all night, worrying and pacing.

***

The next week, Kim checked out five books from the library on abusive relationships and how they work. Carol read three new cookbooks online. Josh read the stocks in the newspaper, in case this wedding led to pawnable wedding gifts and he had any cash to invest afterward.

***

The next week, Carol called crying so hard that Kim couldn't understand anything that she was saying. Kim had to leave work and go over there, just to make sure that Carol didn't need an ambulance or the police.

"He's gone!" Carol screamed in anguish. "The love of my life is gone!"

Kim tried her best not to smile and failed.

"You have to help me try to find him!"

Kim shook her head no, climbed into her Civic, and drove home, smiling the whole way.

***

The next week, Kim was walking around downtown with an ice cream cone and there he was. He was passed out in the back of an open, fully-packed UHaul, clearly someone else's. Kim gasped. He opened his eyes slightly, stared for a moment, and said, "Don't worry – I'm going back to her tomorrow."

"No, you're not."

He opened his eyes fully and glared. "Yes, I am."

Among the high-end furniture and plastic boxes in the truck, there was still an open corner. Kim was immediately possessed by a vision. She walked quickly back to her Civic and grabbed duct tape from her trunk. Then she ran back to the UHaul. He had passed out again while she was gone. She rolled him gently toward the open corner and leaned him up behind a couch. Starting with his wrists and ankles and working as quickly as possible, she used her entire roll of duct tape on him. When she was finished, he was stuck to the back of that couch, unable to get out, unable to scream, and completely invisible to the packers. She jumped out of the back of the truck just in time to see a young couple, standing next to an end table on the sidewalk, both on their cell phones to the police.

She tried to look as innocent as possible when they cuffed her.

***

"Miss Sedlock. Did you ... duct-tape a homeless man ... to the back of a couch ... in someone else's UHaul truck?"

Despite some inappropriate laughter from the other criminals, the arraignment went well. She pled no contest, and since she had no previous record, Kim would pay a fine and be a participant in The Diversion Program. That meant, as long as she paid, the only trace of the incident would be a record that she was arrested. It wouldn't say why. It would say only that the case had been dismissed.

The police gave her a free bus pass for one trip home. She waved goodbye to her cellmates and yelled out some parting advice about always stretching first. They handed her the inmate-numbered plastic bag with her things in it. They gave her privacy to change and she decided to keep her bag, slipping it into her pocket. It had her name on it, right above the inmate number; she would give it to a cute guy.

On the bus stop bench, there was an abandoned newspaper. She flipped through it to see what everyone else in the world had been through while she'd been cooped up in jail. And right there, in the front of the wedding section, was a big, black-and-white, laughing, radiant, glamorous picture of Carol and Josh.

The bus pulled up. It was empty. Kim stared out the window on her way home. As she walked up to her house, she reached into the box on the porch for the mail. There was only one envelope in it, but it was fancy linen stationary, with beautiful cursive, and it was from Carol. She tore it open. The letter contained only one sentence:

Would you like to be my maid of honor?

It was paper-clipped to a fancy wedding invitation.

Kim stared at it for several minutes and then burst into laughter.

But she stopped laughing when she realized that, in a strange way, she was happy just to be included.

11

Blankets

One day Rebecca woke up and realized she had accidentally become a bank-teller. It was supposed to have been a transitional job, a refuge between college life and Her Career That She Hadn't Chosen Yet. That was three years ago. But this polished woman in a blazer – a designer straitjacket, she called it now – had told her that – congratulations! She was bright enough, articulate enough, even professional-seeming. She told her that she would be able to work at the Bank of America as if she had won a national award, as if she was the next contestant on The Price Is Right.

She bought it, too. She listened to the other bank tellers talking about how they were in a far classier area of the city than First National, how Mr. Fitch was famous in the financial world, how their cousins were working at Dunkin' Donuts and oh-so jealous. She wanted to do well. She started worrying about whether her clothes were mature enough, whether she was as personable as Gwen, the teller at the next window, whether everyone liked her or whether they gossiped viciously behind her back, the way they did with the other new girl. And over time, she got comfortable. She could check up on any file she needed to, her arithmetic got faster, so did eight hours a day, and they gave her her own cup in the coffee lounge. She stopped noticing that the job was taking up space in her life. Gradually, she stopped practicing the sax, and then she stopped even feeling guilty about it. She worked and napped and her old friends never called her and she never called them, either. They were scattered across America and she didn't want to know what they were doing – especially not Dana. But every now and then, Dana would skip through her daydreams with a wineglass in one hand and a Pulitzer Prize in the other, and Rebecca would quickly cover her up with a fuzzy white blanket to make her fade into the background of her mind.

And then one night, she dreamt about her. Dana was right in front of her bedroom window, dancing to Howlin' Wolf music in a long black dress that billowed and swirled and blocked Rebecca's view of the daytime clouds. There was energy to Dana's dancing, and she was laughing and tossing her hair around. Rebecca wanted so badly to join her that finally she leapt out of bed and tried to run out of her apartment, but the bedroom door was stuck. She struggled and pushed against it, turning the knob again and again, pushing with her hands and then with her whole arms, and finally with her head, too, until she slid down the door and became a pile on her floor. She could still hear Dana's laughter mixing with the music.

It was hours before the alarm when she sat up, awake. The image of it struck her instantly, as she had seen it on many made-for-television movies: character's dream ends with her sitting up suddenly, sweating – they're *always* sweating after nightmares. She felt her forehead to see how accurate those movies were, but it was dry. Her whole body was dry – chilly, in fact.

She lay there for a while listening to the traffic, and then she went out to the hall closet to get an extra blanket. It wasn't on the shelf, though. She thought maybe it was in the wrong part of the closet, so she started rifling through everything that she never used anymore: two tennis rackets, broken ice skates, a box of yearbooks. Halfway through, she remembered that she had lent the blanket to Mr. Fitch at the bank picnic a month ago and he had never returned it.

Realizing this made Rebecca furious, which was unusual for her. She had not been genuinely furious since she had been living with her parents, but here she was, slamming her tennis rackets against the wall at 3am. She only stopped because of the neighbors.

After that, she continued rifling through her closet. She re-read her yearbooks – not only what everyone had written to her, but everyone's senior quotes and their activities. She looked at a picture of herself lying sideways on a cafeteria table, surrounded by sheet music, propped up on one elbow, smiling at the camera. And a picture of Dana after her first public reading, stuffing the last of the chocolate-covered grapes from the reception into each other's mouths.

Finally, around four, she got to her sax. It was at the very bottom of her closet. She took it out and ran her fingers over it, feeling each key, each hole, each curve. She imagined it was vibrating in her hands. It seemed like she did this for hours, but it was still dark out when she put it in her mouth and blew a C major. She played the blues scales, the jazz arpeggio, Boogie Woogie Bugle Boy (the first song she had ever learned), and then she improvised – that was always the best for her.

Neighbors started banging on her walls, her ceiling, and finally, her door. She forced herself to stop playing, but she didn't answer the door, and when Mrs. Dooly yelled through the crack that her loud music had woke her up, she yelled back, "Yeah, me, too!"

Next it was coffee, lots and lots and lots of coffee, and the butterfly stationary that was hidden under her yearbooks. She wrote to herself first. She wrote the speech that she would give to the woman who hired her and the speech that she would give to Mr. Fitch. Farewell, Fitchface.

Her other letter was to Dana:

Dear Dana,

I'm working at a bank and I haven't touched my sax in a long time before tonight.

But I still want to read your best stories.

Signing it was unnecessary; she would know who it was from.

She found it months later when she was putting back the blanket that Mr. Fitch had returned to her at a staff meeting. It was funny that she didn't recognize her own handwriting at first.

To think, she had almost mailed it.

That night seemed like a long time ago and she had only had one nightmare since. In it, she was throwing a dinner party for her colleagues. They came to her living room in a big group. She told them that she would hang up their coats, but the hallway closet was missing. She kept feeling the wall frantically, as she smiled over her shoulder at them, but the wall was seamless and smooth; there wasn't even a mark on it, and when she turned to them, helplessly, they started taking off their coats, one by one, and piling them on top of her – thick wool coats, soft and comfortable, over her body, over her face until she couldn't see or breathe, and they couldn't see her, either.

Another day, Rebecca woke up and realized she was still a bank-teller and decided to talk it over with Gwen. She didn't know if it was actually a decision, really; it was more like an accident. They were on an hour-long lunch break that day because the new girl was training and Rebecca got a little too relaxed. She told Gwen about Dana and the images she could evoke from thin air, images that were still with her, characters that had broken her heart. She was talking in a way that was very inappropriate and she saw the teller at the next table smile at his lunch partner when she said that Dana owned so much truth. She told Gwen about the blues clubs they had gone to together, the old bald black men jamming in clouds of smoke, how they stayed up all night talking about their futures, how when they were both mildly famous Dana would write the lyrics to her songs. She told all of this to Gwen – Gwen in her tweed suit, who usually talked about the latest financial documentaries and how they were wrong and about sticking to traditional investments – *Gwen* with the smile that no one could tell was a smile. Rebecca told it all to her in the space of fifteen minutes, and afterward, she couldn't believe she had said it.

There was a long silence during which she wanted to run, and then Gwen said that she had been friends with an artist in college, too, but that now her friend was starving and always wanting to borrow money. Rebecca said that was probably the case with Dana as well, but she felt like she was lying, and then she changed the subject. It occurred to Rebecca later that Gwen had never even asked her what instrument she had played.

Eventually, Rebecca was promoted to a position that both easier and vaguer. She got to call her parents about it, she had a party that didn't feel much like a party, and she got an office with a big shiny nameplate.

Another colleague mentioned her twelve-year-old son wanted sax lessons, and she needed to leave before five to go to Music Galaxy, where they sold used instruments in the back. Rebecca told her she could have hers. She had to dust it off first.

She began to avoid bookstores. She became convinced that Dana's brilliant new works would be lining the shelves and she just didn't have time to read them. She recycled another reunion letter, but a few years afterward, there was a small dinner near Rebecca and she spontaneously said yes. She figured it would be alumni that lived near her. She tried on three different outfits before settling on an artsy denim dress that was splattered with embroidery. She was late and nearly running down East Locust Street when she thought that she saw Dana in a red velvet cape, looking up at the sky while she walked. She had on thigh-high leather boots and earphones. Ducking into the restaurant, she realized it had been Dana, that she looked young, and worse, she looked the same. Against all etiquette, Rebecca gasped in horror. She had always feared it, but she never thought it would actually happen. She thought about running out before Dana registered her presence, making a quick turn down a side street before Dana said that she had been in town for years, that she had seen Rebecca running around with her tight bun, her briefcase in one hand, grocery bag in the other. Dana was the only one who would know that she was wearing a ridiculous disguise nearly every day. She meant to do it, just bolt and then duck down a side street, but she couldn't stop watching Dana standing in the seating area. With her long white fingers toying with the fringe on her red velvet cape, she just looked so damn intriguing. Rebecca thought that even if she had never known anything about Dana, she would have looked that way to her in that moment. The secret to living an exotic life was buried within that fringe and Dana's fingers would uncover that secret, use it, then fling it aside and go for more and different secrets.

When Dana saw finally Rebecca, her smile was gradual, beginning in her eyes and travelling outward to the rest of her face until she glowed, and then she was running across the seating area toward Rebecca, throwing her arms around her, kissing her cheeks. Her huge silver hoop earrings kept smacking Rebecca in the face as Rebecca was confronted by Dana's perfume. She had forgotten about her perfume. It was the one thing about her which she had never admired and she was amazed that, after all these years, no one had told her yet how awful it was. It smelled like an odd combination of cleaning chemicals and rotting limes, with maybe a hint of brand new furniture.

Dana began chattering so quickly and dramatically that, having had nothing to say to her a minute ago, Rebecca suddenly felt compelled to interrupt her, but she didn't; she just listened. Dana's long white fingers swept the air so quickly as she spoke that Rebecca could see trails. Seattle was *magical* and this new guy Rick was *brilliant* and this trip to Boston *must have been sent from angels, it was so magical and brilliant!* Dana grabbed Rebecca's hand and said that they must go to a blues club that night, and then she winked. Rebecca had forgotten how she was always winking.

Up to that point, Rebecca was beginning to believe that she might get through this without ever admitting that she had been a bank-worker for the past seven years, but now she realized this was just the beginning. Dana would be in town for four more days. Rebecca spoke to Dana then for the first time since graduation. She said, "Of course, we must!" but her voice came out all muffled and, for a second, Dana squinted at her, but then pushed on with a funny story about her flight.

Somehow, they wound up at Rebecca's apartment together. Rebecca had been so nervous that she talked extra loud as she unlocked the front door just to divert attention away from her shaking hands, but now, after three glasses of wine, she was beginning to feel almost drowsy. They were fake-laughing about the time they gotten locked out of the dorm in their underwear because some loser, whose name neither of them could remember, had played a prank on them, and then Rebecca said it: "I'm an assistant personnel manager at Bank of the States."

Dana looked stunned, but Rebecca tried to will herself not to blush. Dana did not say anything at first and then she launched right into how *marvelous* that was. But there was something a little off about her eyes, the way they kept daring toward the door when she paused. Her voice got high and strained.

Rebecca thought, She's embarrassed the way people are when they accidentally see someone naked. She's embarrassed *for* me – and if she was embarrassed now, in a second she would be more so. She would be forced to tell Rebecca that she was a writer, like she'd always longed to be, and they would be on unequal ground. But it was half over and Rebecca just had to get it done with.

"So what do you do for work?" Rebecca asked her.

Looking back, she should have realized that it was strange for Dana not to have started with these questions when they had first met in the restaurant. Now Rebecca knew why. Dana had been a phone psychic and a waitress for the past seven years and still was. But they were both transitional jobs. She had stopped writing altogether one year after graduation.

Rebecca was mortified, even too mortified to be relieved. She had lost the other half of her dreams, the half by which she measured herself and knew that she was failing, the half that she held up higher than where she could ever be. Dana was not dancing through life, not climbing up a spiral staircase of her most solid images, trusting that they would hold her, trusting that she wouldn't fall. Instead she was trying to forget, just like Rebecca, that there was anything that made her one hundred percent alive, and now that Rebecca knew it, she could see that Dana was looking at things a little less sharply. Dana's world was soft-focus, just like her own, and all of Dana's drama was just trying to mask it. Dana was not feeling anything.

Rebecca wanted to be a good friend to Dana that evening, to tell her what she needed to do to escape, but instead, she treated her the way she treated herself: She lulled her with wine and then wrapped her up in her thickest angora blanket, the kind so thick your nightmares couldn't get through it, she told her, and was sorry she had said even that.

12

The Wide Range of Subtlety Among Us

He spent a lot of time sharpening his daggers. Each one was engraved with an important phrase, right on the blade. "You're not as talented as you think you are", "You have no real friends", "You were a terrible parent", "Your work is meaningless". They weren't phrases he thought about himself; they were phrases he thought about everyone he knew. And when his knives were sharp, he hung them up on his mantle with colored leather cords and they dangled there, until he could no longer hold back, until he had to come out and just tell the person, but instead of saying the words, he drove the knife with that phrase right into their heart and then ran.

She had many things to say to everyone she knew as well. But instead of engraving these things on daggers, she wrote them down on colorful slips of paper and then hid them in her apartment. "You're hurting my feelings", "You're losing my trust", "I am not truly happy", "It's not O.K." After she hid each phrase, she believed and acted as if she had actually told it to that person. And she felt better; she had expressed herself.

They met at a coffee shop. He read her a Shakespearean sonnet and spilled coffee on his journal. She giggled and took a phone pic of him in his crazy hat. They hung out for months, seeing independent films, eating Thai food, and having sex in front of her cats. During that time, she wrote many phrases and hid them. "I am not comfortable with that", "You sound mean", "I don't think you're really listening", "This isn't what I pictured." She hid all of them really well; she couldn't even find them herself anymore. He worked on a new dagger that said "You are not my soulmate", and one night, when she was tipsy on wine and lying on her floor with some throw pillows, he drove it all the way into her.

He didn't realize that the police never paid much attention to the engravings. They were much more concerned with his motives, his methods, his profile. They didn't really care what he had to say; no one did. They all treated the knife as if it were more important than the phrase.

13

Pandemic

The Wakefield Commune was named for its founder Johnny Wakefield, an old farmer and hippie, and it believed in direct giving, as a group. There were sixty-three members, all living on the seemingly endless land, many from wealthy families who had disowned them, some from failed tiny farms, a bunch home-schooling their kids in conflict mediation and biodynamic farming and engineering and music. Often, they were all dressed in the same fabric, not because they were a cult, but because Polly made all their clothes and she would buy the fabric in bulk.

Anyway, their belief in direct giving was rooted in their suspicion that institutions like churches and formal charities were taking away motivating human emotions, re-directing kind impulses that people felt toward each other away from positive action, like giving a twenty dollar bill to a single mom or letting a friend who just had a bad break-up crash on a couch, and toward useless outlets, like buying tote bags with giant earth logos or filling out prayer cards. "The problem," Johnny had said, "is that people are getting the same buzz from these useless gestures as they would from effective actions. They feel great about themselves for wearing pink for Breast Cancer Awareness month. They think that they're Mother Teresa if they give $100 to a stylish-looking charity that will keep $80 of it for their glossy brochures. That euphoric feeling that humans get when they have truly helped another human in need is supposed to be reserved for when you actually make a difference. But what's happening ... it's a form of masturbation. People are masturbating their hearts."

"Well, some of these institutions, like children's hospitals, for example, might close if we don't support them in droves," Jimmy countered. Jimmy was Johnny's younger brother. He didn't live at Wakefield Commune year-round, because his kids were in a great Montessori school in California, but he would come by for the harvest with his guitar and a big bag of weed and he would help as much as his back would allow.

Johnny just looked at Jimmy for a second. Johnny had the kindest eyes of anyone that most people had seen. His eyes alone could relax you and make you feel safe and cared for. "I am not saying that we shouldn't or can't give to children's hospitals, Jimmy. All I'm saying is that we need more direct giving. In addition to group giving, types that are effective, we need one-on-one direct spontaneous giving to people in need. I mean, is that even controversial?"

"No, no, of course not, Johnny. People don't trust each other is the problem. A man says he is down on his luck and has a family to feed and then he takes the money that you give him – that you barely have yourself to give – and he buys another bag of heroin."

"I don't think there's as much of that stuff out there as you think." Johnny sat back and started whittling a piece of wood. "Look at the things we take pride in, Jimmy. Putting on a uniform to kill strangers in other countries for rich people's gain. Inventing a new pill for people who don't want to eat right. Or can't because they never get raises. We feel proud if our favorite team wins. And those things don't have the meaning or the impact that direct giving does. Why don't we harness our positive feelings, consider where they will have the strongest impact, and put them there instead? Standing up and saying that our friends are being mistreated should make us prouder than shooting at impoverished strangers for more fossil fuel. People can learn how to truly help each other, you know. The folks at the very bottom never see any of this charity money that's being thrown around."

"No, I agree, Johnny. One hundred percent. I'm with you."

"We're all getting the feelings of reward without putting in the actual work."

"It's true." But we can't screen who we are helping, Jimmy thought. He knew better than to say that out loud to Johnny, though.

The dinner bell rang then and everyone ran through the fields with their dogs to the stone dining hall to hear Jimmy play some Dylan, to visit with their smaller children, and to munch on roasted corn yet again and that new curry vegetable stew that Lori just invented or downloaded. Everyone was chatting loudly and laughing and singing along with Jimmy. There was a fire and one of the smaller kids was throwing Bergamot flowers into it to watch them burn. They smelled wonderful as they burned.

On The Duchess of Monmouth Cruise Ship, thousands of miles away, they were also having dinner, only theirs was gourmet rack of lamb with candles lit and a brass band in the background. This was where the pandemic would start. Up until this very moment, there were people who gave only to organized charities and never in their personal lives. These people believed they were genuinely helping in the best way possible for them. But it wasn't until the toast given at their dinner that night that the pandemic began to spread contagiously throughout America.

The director of the cruise package sales raised his glass. "We would just like to thank Bags For Babies, a phenomenal charity that has partnered with us. We are honored to have members of their board here with us tonight, and we want to inform everyone that five percent of your dinner profits will go to their amazing organization. This company creates brand-new stylish bags for parents with newborns so that they can carry their baby's supplies with honor and dignity. You will notice the slideshow that has begun to your left. These are families and their babies going to a company-sponsored picnic with their new bags. Notice how much happier and more secure these babies look."

It was at that very moment that everyone present was overtaken with a strange stirring. They would give only to people with slideshows that they could see, to places that produced honor and dignity in their recipients, to funds that were organized and policed by savvy upper-class investors. It seemed at first to be a thought that everyone present happen to share, as a result of hearing the same toast and seeing the same actor-produced slideshow, but it wasn't. It would later be determined in labs that it was viral. A brain infection had spread throughout the cruise ship and when it landed a week later in Seattle, the notion of direct giving would become obsolete in nursing homes, hospitals, and restaurants. The highway would erect a new billboard that read, "If my name ain't on a plaque, I ain't givin' back!" Those who were not infected would be baffled by it, but when they called city hall to complain, they were met with vacant out-of-touch voices that echoed the wisdom of the billboard and then hung up.

The patients in the nursing home were most deeply affected, as they turned away their grandchildren's visits and threw out their inaccurate crayon drawings. "These children cannot expect us to coddle their feelings about their bad art or their stupid conversation when they are not at all organized, give us no recognition for our contributions to them, and have no proof that they deserve our love," one senior told the local news channel. In the background, many seniors yelled out in agreement, pumping their fists in the air in a strange rhythm.

Now, as a group, The Wakefield Commune was not big on following the news. First of all, they were not big fans of the American government, and secondly, they didn't feel that the major issues were really be-ing covered, most of the time. But word of the epidemic had spread to Johnny and he sat by his old radio all day now, listening as it spread across New York State and approached his beloved commune. He didn't mention it to anyone else there. They had no contact with the outside world anyway, except when they brought the harvest to market, and even then, it was only the men. He didn't want to alarm them for no reason, but because he didn't mention it, he could not know if they already knew. Many of them had laptops and the commune itself, although devoid of television, did have Wi-Fi.

Johnny understood that he could not reason with those infected. Sci-entists from every state had determined that there was a change in the patients' brains that conversation could not correct. It was so widespread at this point that the journalists were saying that everyone in New York State would be exposed eventually. Johnny was up all night, sitting on the porch, listening to the crickets, and as he watched the sun rise, he settled on an idea. He needed to make the commune into an organized charity. It was the only way.

He asked to borrow Polly's laptop and he freed up some of their emergency fund. Then he started placing orders. He ordered materials to make glossy brochures and cell phones with high quality cameras to make slideshows. He ordered fancy thank-you notes and complimentary gift bags with ribbons. He hired a stranger to build a website for them and he began the paperwork to become an LLC. Then he went back to the porch and tried to figure out how he would announce this to the commune. Normally, they did everything by consensus and he had not consulted a soul.

He felt a little faint with everyone seated Indian-style on the lawn in front of the porch, with him looming over them, his eyes darting from the children braiding each other's hair to Polly and Lori shucking beans to Jimmy in the front, wiping his spectacles on his shirt and then placing his full attention on Johnny.

"I don't know what you've heard already about this pandemic. It has spread all over the world and, as of now, there is no cure and there is no vaccine. It is a disease that stops people from giving in the moment, from giving from their hearts, from inventing their own giving and following through on it. People who get it can only give through organized charities, and even then, only ones that appeal to them with good advertising and rewards. If we were to get this disease – and it is spreading all over New York State as I speak – then we would also stop believing in direct giving. There would be no way to stop the change in our brains. So I have devised a way for us to get the funds that we need to completely isolate ourselves from society for a long, long time. We need to become an organized charity."

Jimmy jumped to his feet. "How can you say that?! That is against everything that you believe! Against everything that we believe!"

"I know." Johnny hung his head. "But if we survive with our sanity, the world has hope. If we succumb to the disease, it won't matter what we believe."

"You're talking like the decision has already been made," Polly called out.

Johnny could not look up at her. "The decision has already been made."

Everyone started shouting at once. Johnny couldn't tell what responses were coming from where. He went to his bedroom and laid down and did not get up, even for meal time.

After about twenty-four hours, everyone had calmed down. It was a terrifying thought that their beliefs would be changed by this pandemic, so they came to the conclusion that Johnny was right. Their only chance was to become an organized charity, and one that appealed to the masses.

The entire commune appeared in Johnny's bedroom the next day.

"This picture of a kitten will be on the t-shirts," Lori announced, holding up an image on her laptop.

"I wrote our jingle," offered Jimmy.

"Our rewards bags will have French perfume and a matching French perfume for dogs," Polly said with a wry grin. "I am not joking."

In this way, Wakefield Commune became a charity organization with themselves as the charity cases. Some donors enjoyed selecting a particular farmhand to sponsor. Others just wanted picture updates of group projects such as the harvest. The hard part was never allowing the donors to visit and to infect Wakefield Commune with the disease. They had taken down all information about their location and frankly, no one could find them anymore.

In a state of depression that he thought might never lift, Johnny took a walk around the edges of his land. He picked some wildflowers, but that did not cheer him up. He whistled an old tune, but couldn't finish it. He looked for exotic birds and forgot what he was looking for. Finally, a raggedy-looking teenage girl came down the dirt road, all by herself and crying. Johnny ran to meet her. Afraid of being infected, he stopped short ten feet away.

"I don't have it," she said plainly. "I don't have anything anymore."

Johnny ran the rest of the way to her and hugged her. "These are strange times," he said. He could give her a home, food, friends, work, and play. He beamed. He would do that. He put his arm around her and walked her back to the dining hall, whistling his old tune loud and strong.

www.ingramcontent.com/pod-product-compliance
Lightning Source LLC
Chambersburg PA
CBHW070658100726
47907CB00007B/2258